THE
SCIENCE FICTION
PUZZLE BOOK

Published in 2020 by Welbeck

An imprint of Welbeck Non-Fiction Limited,
Part of Welbeck Publishing Group
20 Mortimer Street
London W1T 3JW

A CIP catalogue record for this book
is available from the British Library

ISBN 978-1-78739-488-9

Project Editor: Georgia Goodall
Designer: Eliana Holder
Production: Marion Storz
Picture Research: Paul Langan

10 9 8 7 6 5 4 3 2 1

Printed in Dubai

THE
SCIENCE FICTION
PUZZLE BOOK

INSPIRED BY THE WORKS OF ISAAC ASIMOV, RAY BRADBURY, ARTHUR C CLARKE, ROBERT A HEINLEIN AND URSULA K LE GUIN

TIM DEDOPULOS

WELBECK

CONTENTS

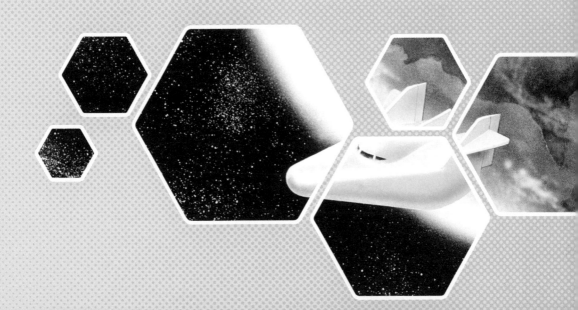

INTRODUCTION

If there is a diamond core to science fiction, then it is the question, "What if?". The genre has always been a lens through which people examine the world and speculate how things might plausibly be different. To quote the great Octavia Butler, "Science fiction frees you to go anyplace and examine anything." The best writers have always looked at society and seen its written and unwritten laws, then played with them.

What if this restriction was ramped up to breaking point?

What if that one no longer existed?

This is a book of puzzles, rather than a book of philosophy, so the questions you'll find in here are a little more pointed. Like SF itself, they range from technically precise to laterally open-ended. Some of them test calculation, some scientific knowledge, some logic and some ingenuity. Every puzzle is inspired by or rooted in a specific SF story, and where the question is more lateral, the answer in the back reflects the story's original solution. You might very well be able to come up with something better!

The authors whose work inspired these puzzles are great indeed – but they are by no means the only great SF authors. Many, many more writers deserve to be included, but physical reality is unforgiving. There isn't even space to list all the names of the authors who should be in here, but if you have not yet done so, please do consider reading Margaret Atwood, Octavia Butler, Samuel R Delany, Philip K Dick, W E B DuBois, Greg Egan, Harry Harrison, Aldous Huxley, Fritz Lieber, George Orwell, Joanna Russ, James Tiptree Jr, H G Wells, John Wyndham and Roger Zelazny. Amongst many others.

Writing puzzles inspired by specific pieces of fiction is a little like cooking. Sometimes, the original material is going to get a bit chopped around. I have sincerely tried to stay true to the stories and still keep the actual questions relevant. I have had to take some definite liberties, however, so please do not judge the authors in here by my pale reflections.

In a universe of infinite variety, every wonder and marvel is not just possible, but certain. Science fiction is the gateway to that universe, and it's as easy to step through as picking up a book or an e-reader. Come inside and let 'What if?' show you sights you'd never dreamed possible.

Tim Dedopulos

ISAAC
ASIMOV
1920 - 1992

ASIMOV'S
BIOGRAPHY

ISAAC ASIMOV WAS A PROFESSOR OF BIOCHEMISTRY AND ONE OF THE "BIG THREE" SCIENCE-FICTION WRITERS OF THE MID-20TH CENTURY. HE IS BEST KNOWN FOR HIS FOUNDATION SERIES, WHICH WON THE HUGO AWARD FOR "BEST ALL-TIME SERIES". HOWEVER, HE ALSO WROTE THE GALACTIC EMPIRE AND ROBOT SERIES, AS WELL AS NEARLY 500 OTHER BOOKS ACROSS A HUGE RANGE OF GENRES AND NON-FICTION CATEGORIES. THE SELECT BIBLIOGRAPHY OPPOSITE IS MERELY THE TIP OF THE ICEBERG.

An avid teenage consumer of sci-fi stories, he wrote his first story at the age of 17. It was rejected for publication by John W Campbell, the then-editor of *Astounding Science Fiction* and one of the leading sci-fi writers of the time, but it came with advice and mentorship from Campbell himself. His first published story, "Marooned off Vesta", appeared just two years later.

His gift was to take hard science – of which he had a supreme understanding – and make it not just accessible to the average reader, but incredibly interesting, too. His three laws of robotics, which inspired many of his works, have become so accepted that in some circles there is a belief that real robots will one day be designed to their specifications. Whether that happens or not, he has already left an indelible mark on this world and beyond; alongside numerous literary awards named in his honour, an asteroid and a crater on Mars also bear his name.

ISAAC ASIMOV'S SELECTED SCIENCE-FICTION BIBLIOGRAPHY

The Foundation Trilogy

Foundation

Foundation and Empire

Second Foundation

Extended Foundation Series

Prelude to Foundation

Forward the Foundation

Foundation's Edge

Foundation and Earth

The Robot Series

The Caves of Steel

The Naked Sun

The Robots of Dawn

Robots and Empire

Galactic Empire Series

The Currents of Space

The Stars, Like Dust

Pebble in the Sky

Select Other Novels

The End of Eternity

The Gods Themselves

Nightfall

Select Short Stories

I, Robot

The Bicentennial Man and Other Stories

The Complete Robot

ROBOT

ISAAC ASIMOV'S THREE LAWS OF ROBOTICS ARE SOME OF THE MOST FAMOUS AND ENDURING MAXIMS IN ALL OF SCIENCE FICTION. THEY ARE:

THE FIRST LAW: A robot may not injure a human being or, through inaction, allow a human being to come to harm.

THE SECOND LAW: A robot must obey the orders given it by human beings except where such orders would conflict with the First Law.

THE THIRD LAW: A robot must protect its own existence as long as such protection does not conflict with the First or Second Laws.

A research station was testing a form of radiation that was mildly harmful to humans, but fatal to robots in 60 seconds. Unfortunately, any time a scientist performed a test, nearby robots that knew enough to be any use whatsoever would obey their First Law, dash in to prevent harm to the scientist, and either be destroyed or force the scientist to stop the test. So the director changed their programming to remove "or, through inaction, allow a human being to come to harm" from the First Law.

One of these modified robots became accidentally fixated on an annoyed researcher's command to "get lost!" and hid in a batch of brand new robots that are unmodified and know nothing about the station. These robots are identical to the rogue robot in every physical way. The rogue will not obey any new commands and is doing everything permitted by its programming to remain lost, including making the choice to obey the original version of the First Law.

WHAT ORDERS DO YOU GIVE THAT WILL FORCE THE ROBOT TO REVEAL ITSELF?

ANSWER
PG/170

ANSWER PG/170

13

MARS

During an epidemic of a particularly virulent, untreatable and unkillable Martian plague, a patient arrives at a medical station badly injured. They are in immediate need of three operations, one from each of the three surviving surgeons, A, B and C. The patient may or may not be infected, and the same is true of the surgeons. There are no symptoms before the moment of death. The plague is virulent, and passes instantly by touch, skin to skin, skin to object, and object to object, indefinitely. This is, at least, the only way it can be passed.

Unfortunately, because of the paranoia engendered by the plague, genuinely protective medical gloves have become a desperately sought commodity, and there are only two pairs available. There are plenty of duplicates of all other required materials.

It is possible to put on, remove, and invert the gloves with sterile tools, so assume that no one has to touch the gloves at all in order to put them on or take them off. However, if a surgeon is infected, the plague will transfer from them to the inside of the gloves. Likewise, if the patient is infected, it will pass from their skin to the outside of the gloves. The gloves cannot be sterilized again, and all three surgeries require both hands.

HOW CAN THE SURGEONS USE THE GLOVES IN ORDER TO ENSURE THAT IT IS IMPOSSIBLE TO CONTAMINATE - OR BE CONTAMINATED BY - EITHER EACH OTHER OR THE PATIENT?

ANSWER PG/170

WIDOWER

A widower discovers that a significant amount of cash, as well as a number of valuable bearer bonds, has been stolen from the company he owns. There is only one other person who knows how to access the safe – his nephew, who serves as his chief financial officer. The nephew has an unusual quirk in that he only ever speaks the truth, no matter the personal cost to himself. He is not a pleasant or popular man, but his word is absolutely reliable.

The widower seeks out his nephew and tells him that money and bonds were stolen from the safe the previous night. Then he confronts him and demands to know if he was involved or even fully responsible.

The nephew's answer is swift and certain. "I have never revealed how to access the safe in any manner. I have never helped anyone to rob the company. I did not take the cash or the bonds."

The widower apologizes for asking and leaves. But as the police investigation into the theft drags on, and the days turn to weeks, he starts to wonder. However, his nephew's truthfulness is unassailable.

EVEN SO, IS IT POSSIBLE THAT THE MAN REALLY DID COMMIT THE THEFT?

16

ANSWER
PG/171

ALIENS

In one of his essays, Asimov wrote, "One of the questions that is asked innumerable times these daring days (I have even asked it myself) is: 'If there is life elsewhere in the Universe, why hasn't it reached us?'"

This question is known as the Fermi Paradox, after the legendary physicist who posed it to a couple of colleagues over lunch one day. After all, there are hundreds of billions of stars in our galaxy, and probably trillions of planets. The Sun is fairly young, so there's every possibility that there are intelligent civilizations who are billions of years old. Going by our own technological development, and by the way that exponential growth works, that ought to be plenty of time to have colonized the entire galaxy.

Aliens should be a normal facet of daily life on Earth. So where are they? It's not really a paradox, of course. We just don't know the answer.

Some religious or sceptical people take the Fermi Paradox as proof that there is no intelligent extra-terrestrial life – they aren't here because they aren't anywhere. Many others posit a "Great Filter", a technological or social misstep that invariably kills off all intelligent species. It's certainly a possibility.

CAN YOU THINK OF ANY OTHER REASONS WHY THEY AREN'T HERE?

ANSWER
PG/171

LOGIC

Logic is one of the most vital pillars of all scientific advancement. Without it, we falter and collapse into superstition and guesswork. It is a precise framework that supports some of our most startlingly elegant deductions.

Complete the table below using only the decimal digits from one to nine, so that each gap contains an entry, and every statement is complete and accurate.

IN THIS TABLE, THERE ARE:

- [ ] INSTANCE(S) OF THE NUMBER 1;

- [ ] INSTANCE(S) OF THE NUMBER 2;

- [ ] INSTANCE(S) OF THE NUMBER 3;

- [ ] INSTANCE(S) OF THE NUMBER 4; AND

- [ ] INSTANCE(S) OF THE NUMBER 5.

ANSWER
PG/172

SOLAR

WE ALL KNOW THAT THE EARTH MOVES IN A BROADLY CIRCULAR PATH AROUND THE SUN, WHICH STAYS MORE OR LESS STILL. RIGHT?

WRONG.

DESCRIBE THE EARTH'S ACTUAL PATH.

ANSWER
PG/173

EMPIRICAL

The planet Trantor is the closest planet to the centre of the Milky Way galaxy that is habitable by humans. It was settled by humans around 10,000CE, after our discovery of hyperspace technology. Initially the hub of a small republic of just five worlds, the planet grew into an important regional confederation, and eventually a galaxy-spanning Empire.

Earth had become radioactive by this time, but much of the knowledge and culture of pre-space human society had been retained. A person from our time visiting Trantor would, of course, be astonished to find a planet that was completely covered by one huge city, shielded from the dreadful weather by artificial domes. But once acclimatized to the technological marvels, it would not be so hard to fit in.

BUT NOT EVERYTHING FROM EARTH MADE IT TO TRANTOR. ONE NOTABLE OMISSION FROM THE TRANTORIAN EMPIRE IS THE USE OF AND REFERENCE TO THE ASTRONOMICAL CONSTELLATIONS. DO YOU KNOW WHY? THE DOMES ARE TRANSPARENT.

ANSWER
PG/173

PULL

Depending on how you define it, escaping the Earth is a thing that happens at very different distances. On the pettiest level, you're briefly escaping the Earth every time you run or jump. The outer edge of the mesosphere, about 50 miles out, is where meteors enter the atmosphere enough to start burning up. Is getting past that point enough of an escape for you? The exosphere is where most of our artificial satellites are placed. It starts a few hundred miles from the surface and runs all the way to more than 6,000 miles out, the point where the last shreds of our atmosphere end, and the solar wind begins.

But that's just the physical atmosphere. Earth's magnetic field has a far greater reach, and its zone of influence – the magnetosphere – shields us from the solar wind. On our day side, the solar wind compresses the magnetosphere to just 40,000 miles of thickness. On the night side, however, in the lee of the solar wind, the magnetosphere stretches out almost 4,000,000 miles – many times further than the Moon, which is a little less than 240,000 miles away.

GIVEN WHAT YOU KNOW OF THE LAWS OF PHYSICS, HOW FAR DO YOU HAVE TO GO TO BE COMPLETELY FREE OF THE EARTH'S GRAVITY?

ANSWER
PG/174

BELT

It is common in science fiction for spaceships travelling around the solar system to fall foul of debris in the asteroid belt, which occupies a big chunk of space between Mars and Jupiter. That seems like a reasonable danger, until you consider that the asteroids are, in fact, thinly spread, and collisions between reasonably big ones – 6 miles in diameter or more – only happen once every 10 million years or so.

So, in reality, the asteroid belt is a safe place to fly a spaceship through. If you actually wanted to collide with a chunk of rock, you'd have to hunt one down and deliberately aim at it.

However, let's pretend the asteroid belt really is the sort of whirling ballet of deadly, closely-packed material familiar to us from stories. You need to make the physical journey from Mars to Jupiter in a very basic spaceship. This means you can't use weapons to clear your path, and your spaceship is completely lacking any shielding, force field or other form of asteroid protection.

HOW DO YOU DEAL WITH THIS IMPOSSIBLY DEADLY ASTEROID BELT?

ANSWER
PG/174

AZAZEL

Slightly under two inches in height and coloured lavender, Azazel was a demon. Or possibly an alien, depending on which of his claims you believed. He agreed to help a man known as Griswold to extract revenge on Felix Hammock, an extremely rich collector of masterwork paintings.

Griswold's complaint was that an idea he had given Hammock for a pittance had made the man 10 million dollars, but Hammock refused to share this profit. Azazel agreed to steal anything that Griswold specified from the collector. Repeat trips back and forth were out of the question, and so was inflicting physical harm on Hammock, but the main constraint was size – being tiny, Azazel could steal a maximum of two grams of matter, barely a fourteenth of an ounce. Even the hole left by stealing a piece of canvas from the centre of one of the collector's Picassos would represent negligible financial harm.

Nevertheless, Griswold managed to come up with a plan whereby Azazel's theft would cut at least 10 million dollars off the value of Hammock's collection, and without causing any damage outside of the removal of the two grams of matter that were stolen.

HOW?

ANSWER
PG/175

VESTA

After the captain of the *Silver Queen* unwisely pursued a course through the asteroid belt, there were just three survivors: Warren, Mark and Michael. There was only a fragment of the spaceship left, consisting of just three airtight rooms and some assorted wreckage connected to them. Between them, the survivors had one spacesuit, a tank containing a year's worth of water, a week of food spread across the various rooms and their cupboards, but only three days of air.

The fragment was in orbit around the asteroid Vesta. The second-largest asteroid in the belt after Ceres, Vesta did have a small, manned station, but the community didn't have their own spaceship and the nearest potential rescuer was a week away. The sealed rooms were

lit and remained at survivable temperature, but the wreckage was otherwise unpowered, with no gas canisters or other potential fuel sources.

The situation seemed bleak until one of the men had an idea. Soon they were headed towards a bumpy landing on Vesta, where people from the station would be able to bring them in safely.

HOW?

ANSWER
PG/175

SILICONY

The space freighter *Robert Q* is critically damaged at Station Five. The crew are killed outright and the alien creature they have with them is fatally injured. It is a silicony, one of a race of beings that live on the surface of asteroids and feed on gamma radiation. Normally they only get to an inch or two in size, but this one is a foot across, and it confirms that the *Robert Q*'s crew had discovered a hugely valuable uranium deposit.

Presumably fearing theft, the crew did not keep a record of the uranium's location inside the ship, nor did they keep it on their persons. There were no flight logs or other forms of locational information to even help trace their route. The silicony could communicate in limited English, and before it died it said that the coordinates of its home deposit were recorded on the asteroid.

ARMED WITH THIS KNOWLEDGE, INVESTIGATOR WENDELL URTH WAS ABLE TO IDENTIFY THE LOCATION OF THE DEPOSIT ON HIS OWN, WITHOUT LEAVING STATION FIVE. HOW?

ANSWER
PG/176

27

GOOSE

American scientists were extremely excited to discover a living goose that laid golden eggs through a catalytic process that converted oxygen-18, a minor isotope of oxygen found in trace amounts in air, to gold. Although the gold was nice, what was more important was that the bird was immune to the radioactivity produced in this conversion. In fact, its process could potentially convert any radioactive isotope to a stable one. If the goose's method of converting oxygen-18 could be understood, the benefits in eliminating nuclear waste alone would be almost incalculable.

The scientists quickly realized that, to learn more, they would need to study developing embryos from the goose, which would mean viable eggs. The eggs, however, were gold. Even keeping the goose in dangerously thin air, there was still enough gold deposited into the eggs to make them sterile. Harming the incredible creature was, of course, out of the question.

CAN YOU THINK OF A WAY TO GET VIABLE EGGS FROM THE GOOSE?

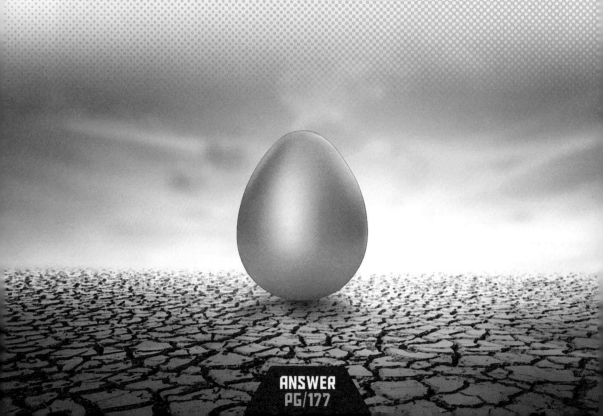

ANSWER
PG/177

HENRY

Mr Jackson is unfailingly honest and absolutely law-abiding, regardless of the personal costs involved in following his strict moral code. Unfortunately, the man he goes into business with, Mr Anderson, is a thief, liar and swindler. It doesn't take long for Anderson to find a way to force Jackson out of the company they start, minus all of his capital.

One evening shortly afterwards, Anderson gets home to discover that Jackson is inside. The man watches in astonishment from a hidden vantage point as Jackson furtively leaves the house, checking for witnesses all the while. Anderson's home is a cluttered treasure trove of valuables of all shapes and sizes, some of them deeply incriminating, but it holds nothing stolen or borrowed from Jackson that the man might plausibly claim legal ownership of, not even a pencil. There is nothing of potentially public ownership there that he could take either, but if there had been, that would not have been a theft. However, Anderson doesn't keep a catalogue of his trove, and even an investigator cannot help him discover what it was that Jackson stole. Increasingly paranoid, the crook goes into a steep decline.

Questioned about the matter years later by the investigator Anderson had briefly retained, Henry Jackson insists that he remained completely true to his code throughout the affair. He confesses that he did, however, steal something from Anderson.

WHAT DID HE TAKE?

ANSWER
PG/177

PAPER

Professor Drake is certain that one of his students, a youth named Lance, has cheated on the final exam for the course in order to get a historically high score.

Security for the examination process at the university is absolutely airtight. A group of proctors watch the professors compile their examination questions – but do not observe the questions themselves – then take the sealed papers away and store them in a high-security safe. It is impossible to spy on the compilation process, to get a look at the paper before it is locked away, or to get to it once it has been secured. On the morning of the examination, once the students are all present at the examination hall, the papers are removed, duplicated and distributed.

The professor would never risk termination by revealing the paper's questions to a student. In fact, outside of compiling the exam under secure conditions, Professor Drake did not write about, speak of or otherwise reveal the questions at any time. He did not even dwell on them mentally. No telepathy or time travel existed at that time, and Lance was not able to become incorporeal or invisible in any way.

NEVERTHELESS, THE PROFESSOR IS RIGHT, AND LANCE DID INDEED CHEAT COMPREHENSIVELY. HOW?

ANSWER
PG/177

MAYOR

Stephen Byerley, an upstanding district attorney in a major city, decides to run for mayor. He has never sought the death penalty and claims to never prosecute an innocent man. He is also famously private, never eating, using the bathroom, or even dozing in public. His opponent, Francis Quinn, begins claiming that Byerley is a robot, and soon the controversy becomes the only issue of the election.

Various tests fail to settle the matter. Byerley eats some apple, but Dr Susan Calvin of US Robots points out that a robot could possess a food pouch in its torso. Quinn attempts to X-ray his opponent secretly, but it turns out the DA wears an X-ray blocker to uphold his right to privacy. Dr Calvin agrees that Byerley's pacifistic stance as DA would be consistent with obeying the First Law of Robotics, but points out it could also just be morality. Byerley does not automatically follow the Second Law, to obey orders from humans, but might have a pre-existing human order overriding new orders.

Eventually, during a stump speech to a hostile audience, a heckler jumps out of the crowd and onto the stage and demands that Byerley punch him in the face. The DA agrees, and does so. The so-called Zeroth Law has not yet been formulated; there is no wiggle room to allow a robot to harm a human in order to benefit humanity at large. Through such a clear violation of the First Law, Byerley conclusively proves that he is not a robot.

HOWEVER, LATER, DR CALVIN ADMITS TO BYERLEY THAT SHE STILL SUSPECTS HIM OF BEING A ROBOT. WHY?

ANSWER
PG/178

PAST

The chronoscope is an invention that allows the user to look directly into the past of any location on Earth. It is rigidly controlled by the government, who, on the rare occasions they deign to provide anything, grudgingly answer questions about the past from scientists and investigators on a rigid item-by-item basis. There is no appeal or explanation for denied requests.

Professor Potterly, an expert on the ancient city-state of Carthage, is so enraged by the constant refusals to grant him answers that he begins looking into creating his own chronoscope – a deeply illegal course of action. Chronoscopy is a forbidden field of research. He quietly recruits some equally rebellious colleagues, and after some time, they come up with a design for an improved device that is both smaller and easy to construct.

The group quickly discover that there is a hard limit to how far back the chronoscope can see – just 120 years. This isn't a flaw with their design, it's a fundamental universal constraint. This proves beyond question that a lot of the government's chronoscope answers are simply lies. They are even more incensed and write up a fully detailed paper for distribution. This outlines the deception and includes plans that allow readers to make their own device.

Government agents arrest them all, but it's too late. The paper has already gone to a whole range of publicity outlets. When the lead agent discovers this, he despairingly points out that the government was only ever trying to keep society safe.

FROM WHAT?

**ANSWER
PG/178**

INFILTRATORS

An American secret agent returns from a deep-cover mission in Russia with horrifying news. The Soviets have developed robots well in advance of American technology — good enough to perfectly mimic specific humans, right down to verbal tics and thought patterns. But that isn't the worst part. Ten of these robots have already quietly replaced American citizens over the last few months, and each functions as part of a total conversion bomb. When the ten come together, they will trigger a nuclear-grade explosion.

Working with just the secret agent, the bureau head organizes an urgent conference of the country's top scientists and thought leaders from across the scientific spectrum in order to figure out how to deal with this emergency. Then, as the first of the chosen delegates is about to arrive, the head realizes that his response was predictable, and the conference itself could be the target. Killing all of the nation's top scientists would be a crippling blow. He prepares orders for the security team to ensure that all delegates are separated and screened before entry.

ALMOST IMMEDIATELY, THE BUREAU HEAD STARTS RECEIVING HORRIFYING REPORTS OF DELEGATES EXPLODING. WHAT IS HIS NEXT MOVE?

ANSWER
PG/179

CONFLICT

As discussed earlier in this book, Asimov's First Law of Robotics states that a robot may not injure a human being or, through inaction, allow a human being to come to harm. The Second Law states that a robot must obey the orders given to it by human beings except where such orders would conflict with the First Law. The Third Law states that a robot must protect its own existence as long as such protection does not conflict with the First or Second Laws. Meddling with these laws is always risky.

An unusually expensive robot nicknamed Speedy had its Third Law strengthened to help prevent casual damage. On Mercury, while helping reboot a mining station, one of the humans gave Speedy a lightly-worded order to retrieve some selenium from a crater. Unfortunately, the crater also contained a source of radiation moderately harmful to the robot. Normally, it would have fetched the selenium anyway, but the poorly-phrased order and the strong Third Law caused a critical conflict and Speedy became trapped circling the crater, unable to process any further orders.

With no way to reboot or shut down the robot, and no available means of communication with it, there seemed to be no solution. The selenium was needed urgently to maintain the station's life support systems, but the original order had not mentioned that, and Speedy was now incapable of understanding that fact. With little time to spare, engineer Mike Donovan managed to find a way to override the critical conflict.

HOW?

ANSWER
PG/179

ASIMOV

HOW MUCH DO YOU KNOW ABOUT ISAAC ASIMOV AND HIS WORKS?

A. Where was Asimov born?
i. America.   **ii.** Britain.
iii. Germany.   **iv.** Russia.

B. In which American city did Asimov grow up?
i. El Paso.   **ii.** Los Angeles.
iii. New York.   **iv.** San Francisco.

C. What mode of travel was Asimov phobic of?
i. Cycling.   **ii.** Driving.
iii. Flying.   **iv.** Sailing.

D. Which one of the following subject classes did Asimov's writing never get published in?
i. Arts.   **ii.** Philosophy.
iii. Religion.   **iv.** Social Sciences.

E. Which of the following environments did Asimov have an unusual love of?
i. Enclosed spaces.   **ii.** High places.
iii. Germany.   **iv.** Wide, open spaces.

F. Which of the following characters works for US Robots as a robopsychologist?
i. Susan Calvin.   **ii.** Mike Donovan.
iii. Alfred Lanning.   **iv.** Greg Powell.

G. Hari Seldon pioneered which field of science?
i. Hyperspace travel.   **ii.** Mind-reading.
iii. Positronics.   **iv.** Psychohistory.

H. In the future of the *Empire* and *Foundation* series, what is wrong with the Earth?
i. Dimensionally unstable. **ii.** Fully paved over.
iii. Radioactive.   **iv.** Too overcrowded.

I. What type of stories involve the Black Widowers?
i. Fantasy.   **ii.** Mystery.
iii. Thriller.   **iv.** Science fiction.

J. What was space ranger David Starr's nickname?
i. Bright.   **ii.** Lucky.
iii. Radio.   **iv.** Super.

ANSWER PG/179

ROBERT A HEINLEIN

1907 - 1988

HEINLEIN'S
BIOGRAPHY

ROBERT A HEINLEIN WAS AN AMERICAN NAVAL OFFICER, AERONAUTICAL ENGINEER AND SCIENCE-FICTION AUTHOR WHO WAS ANOTHER MEMBER OF THE "BIG THREE", ALONGSIDE ASIMOV AND CLARKE. HE WAS A STICKLER FOR SCIENTIFIC ACCURACY IN HIS STORIES AND BECAME A PIONEER OF THE HARD SCIENCE-FICTION SUBGENRE.

Heinlein came to writing in his thirties after being forced to retire from the military due to ill health (it was during this period that he came up with a design for a therapeutic waterbed, which became a feature of some of his later stories). His novels often explored provocative social and political ideas, speculating on how humanity might develop under certain political and communal frameworks. No subject was taboo – he explored race, religion and sexuality within his works. His first foray into this more serious field was his controversial and well-loved title *Starship Troopers*, in which he examines militarism and duty to the state, alongside a gripping storyline. The novel also invented the idea of the "space marine" with mechanized armour.

The sophistication of his work has been recognised extensively with awards and acclaim. Four of his novels won Hugo Awards, and seven were awarded with Retro-Hugos – given to titles published prior to the advent of the award. In 1975, he was named the Science Fiction and Fantasy Writers of America's very first Grand Master.

ROBERT A HEINLEIN'S SELECTED SCIENCE-FICTION BIBLIOGRAPHY

Select Early Novels

The Puppet Masters

Tunnel in the Sky

Double Star

Citizen of the Galaxy

The Door into Summer

Have Space Suit – Will Travel

Methuselah's Children

Starship Troopers

Middle Novels

Strangers in a Strange Land

Podkayne of Mars

Orphans of the Sky

Glory Road

Farnham's Freehold

The Moon is a Harsh Mistress

I Will Fear No Evil

Time Enough for Love

Late Novels

The Number of the Beast

Friday

Job: A Comedy of Justice

The Cat Who Walks Through Walls

To Sail Beyond the Sunset

STOBOR

Humanity has colonized distant planets with the help of interstellar teleportation. The process is instant but expensive, so colonists typically make do with old frontier technology until they have developed far enough for trade to be profitable. Would-be colonists are given extensive training, and before they qualify they are sent on a short solo survival mission to one of a number of unsettled planets.

The last warning that each trainee receives, in the moment before they make the jump, is a concerned instruction to beware of Stobor.

When they return, the newly qualified settlers are informed that Stobor does not, in fact, mean anything. It's just "robots" backwards, and robots – even backwards ones – are not a threat on any planet.

SO WHY THE WARNING?

ANSWER
PG/180

TWINS

The Long-Range Foundation is an organization devoted to space exploration using torch-ships that travel at close to the speed of light. Because of the difficulties of communication across vast distances, the Foundation works with telepaths – specifically, pairs of twins, who because of their close bond are able to communicate instantaneously, mind to mind.

Pat and Tom Bartlett are one of the twin pairs who agree to work with the LRF. Tom ends up joining the crew of a torch-ship, while Pat remains behind on Earth.

From the point of view of Tom and the people on the torch-ship, the Earth is receding at close to the speed of light. From Pat's, the torch-ship is departing Earth at the same speed. Taken from the point of view of a fixed point in space, both the Earth and the torch-ship are moving extremely fast through the universe in their own rights.

TIME DOES STRANGE THINGS AT VERY HIGH SPEED, AND ONE OF THE TWINS WILL AGE FAR FASTER THAN THE OTHER, BUT CAN YOU SAY WHICH?

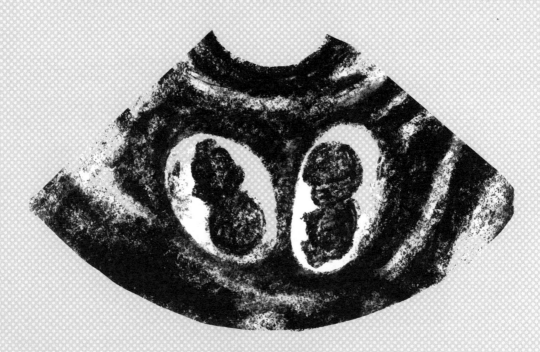

ANSWER
PG/180

GRAND

The Grand Hotel has an infinite number of rooms, all accessed via a portal from the impressive main lobby, which is decorated in lavish Victorian style. Naturally, both the portal and the lobby are able to accommodate an infinite number of guests at any one time, so as to avoid inconvenience.

On one particular evening, the Grand is already holding an infinite number of guests, but an infinite coach arrives, containing an infinite number of new customers who all want their own room. After a moment of thought, the manager decides that the new arrivals can be accommodated without asking any of the current guests to leave the hotel.

HOW?

ANSWER
PG/181

FAMILY

The Howard Families were a group of extremely long-lived bloodlines brought together to intermarry by wealthy philanthropist Ira Howard. The Howard Foundation's hope was that longevity was a trait that could be strengthened through selective breeding, and indeed, this proved to be the case. The best-known member of the Families, Lazarus Long, once said that his natural lifespan was estimated to be around 250 years, but in the end, with the aid of occasional applications of rejuvenation technology, he lived well over two millennia.

Between the constant intermarriage and the very long-lived family members, biological ancestry inevitably became quite a tangled concept within the Howard Families, leading to a number of complicated relationships.

For example, Diana Sperling was the third cousin once removed to Carrie Johnson, on Carrie's mother's side.

SO WHAT RELATION WAS DIANA'S GRANDMOTHER, ANNE, TO CARRIE'S NEWBORN SON, ROBERT?

ANSWER
PG/181

DUST

Many planets of the solar system are settled, and tensions are high between the various worlds. Teenage native Martians Clark and Podkayne Fries, in the company of their Uncle Tom, a senator, are scheduled to take a trip from Mars to Earth. Before departure, Clark is paid to include a package in his luggage, which he is told is a present for the captain. Although he doesn't believe this, he nevertheless takes the package to smuggle aboard the spaceship.

As part of the boarding process, the Fries have to go through a customs screening. When asked if they have anything to declare, Clark sarcastically tells the officer that he's carrying two kilos of a deeply illegal narcotic, happy dust.

PREDICTABLY, CLARK AND HIS LUGGAGE ARE TAKEN ASIDE AND THOROUGHLY AND UNPLEASANTLY SEARCHED. WHY DID HE RISK BAITING THE OFFICER?

ANSWER
PG/182

GRAVITY

Although a lack of Earth gravity is perfectly manageable for short, or even medium, periods of time, it's deeply problematic for longer space journeys. Even setting aside the complexity of equipment and daily life, the body attempts to adapt to the new environment, eroding bone, weakening muscles and more besides. Because of this, extended periods in space require artificial gravity.

Gravity, however, is a function of mass. It's not easily feasible to create a spaceship as dense as the Earth and make it move through the Universe. In some futures, exotic technologies are able to provide specially generated fields of gravity for a spaceship's occupants without damaging or otherwise fouling the ship. Exotic future technology can be a truly magical thing.

IN THE ABSENCE OF SUCH MIRACLES, LESS INNOVATIVE REPLACEMENTS FOR GRAVITY'S PULL ARE REQUIRED. WHAT IS THE SIMPLEST FOR AN ARBITRARILY LONG JOURNEY?

ANSWER
PG/182

CURIOSITY

Estrellita and José were discovered by Lazarus Long on the planet Blessed, for sale in a slave market. Wishing to free them, Long purchased and manumitted the pair, taking them off-planet and giving them the education they had never been permitted. In time, once they were ready for it, he left them to make a life for themselves as free people.

The trader's claim was that the pair were twins, having the same parents and being born from the same pregnancy. Indeed, each child's genetic make-up could be clearly shown to come from the two parents. But despite this, they shared no more genetic similarity than any two random human strangers might do, well outside the possible range of dissimilarity for two siblings.

HOW MIGHT SUCH A THING BE POSSIBLE?

ANSWER
PG/183

LUX

Working together, doctors Archibald Douglas and Mary-Lou Martin come up with a practical, reasonably simple "light panel" that turns electric current directly into light with remarkable efficiency. A little further experimentation shows that the panels also function in the other direction – they can equally efficiently turn light directly into electricity.

Obviously, their discovery has the potential to completely reshape the world's supply of electric power. As they work to bring the devices to market, they come to the attention of the Power Syndicate, a group of power generation companies – oil, hydroelectric, coal, gas and so on – who currently monopolize the entire industry.

The Power Syndicate is incredibly wealthy and immensely, well, powerful. They are determined to ensure that the device can never become a viable product, working to sabotage every stage of the process from distribution and construction right down to obtaining a patent. With the resources available to the Syndicate, there is literally no way that doctors Douglas and Martin – acclaimed scientists, but nothing more – can fend off the cartel.

NEVERTHELESS, THEY STILL BEAT THE SYNDICATE WITHOUT ANY EXTERNAL ASSISTANCE. HOW?

ANSWER
PG/183

TRIFLE

The Cosmic Construction Corps is a military organization that offers the out-of-work youngsters of Earth an avenue for employment and meaning, helping to prepare the rest of the solar system for proper colonization. Andrew Jackson Libby, a poor young Arizona man, has little education and no prospects in the American theocracy of Nehemiah Scudder's Second Revolution, and he gravitates to the Corps. They discover that the young man is, in fact, a mathematical prodigy, and put him to work on a variety of problems.

Common issues for the Corps include matters such as orbital mechanics, rocketry and ballistics. Given the huge range of potential environmental factors contained within the solar system and its bodies – levels of gravity, densities of atmospheres, residual temperatures, stabilities and so on – finding answers to problems of these sorts rapidly becomes incredibly complex.

As a very simple example, imagine a powerful rifle set up on a very large flat plane that is in a vacuum, but is otherwise Earth-like, including identical gravity. With the barrel aiming upwards at 45 degrees for maximum distance, the rifle is strong enough that a bullet fired from the barrel will travel almost 40km before it finally hits the ground.

Now assume that normal sea-level Earth atmosphere is introduced to the plane. Nothing else is changed, and there is no wind, just still air. The same rifle fires a second round, identical in every way to the first.

ROUGHLY SPEAKING, HOW FAR DO YOU THINK THE BULLET WILL GO BEFORE HITTING THE GROUND THIS TIME?

ANSWER
PG/183

ROLLING

In the future, America has replaced its major transportation systems with roadtowns: huge, urbanized platforms that move passengers and goods around at up to 100mph. The roadtowns are maintained by two groups of workers: military engineers and civilian technicians. Because of their lower status, the nuts-and-bolts technicians resent the more white-collar engineers. The Chief Deputy Engineer of the Sacramento sector is named Van Kleeck. An ambitious man, Van Kleeck has full access to both engineering and technical – plans, files, timetables, reports and everything else. He begins giving speeches stoking the technicians' resentment, pretending to empathize with them and building himself a power base.

In time, he gains sufficient influence in his region to launch a campaign for political power. His followers sabotage one of the roadtowns, killing hundreds to demonstrate that the technicians are more important than the engineers, and demanding full control of the region. As efforts continue to defuse the situation, the authorities struggle to understand how Van Kleeck could have recruited so many technicians to his cause. The technicians were all psychologically evaluated in detail as a matter of course before starting work, to weed out subversives and rebellion-prone individuals.

HOW HAS THE MAN MANAGED TO SWAY SO MANY THEORETICALLY SENSIBLE, PRACTICAL PEOPLE?

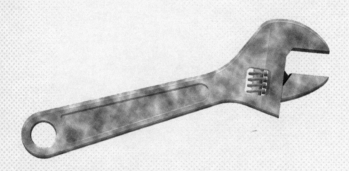

ANSWER
PG/184

ROUTING

Although it is fast, comfortable and efficient, the roadtown system is still a network of points, connected by fixed paths. As such, it is an improvement on the railways and highways it replaced, but it is not a substantial change in core principle.

The single biggest problem with any network of destinations is complexity. If you want to get from A to B, then navigating a large network is not a problem, provided that both points are accessible from that network. You just consider the possible routes between the two and decide which is best for you – the shortest, generally. In a very large network, there might be a lot of possible routes, but there are plenty of ways to eliminate the more inefficient options (such as heading away from your destination) and just compare the more viable ones.

Besides, you only have to calculate the best path from A to B once. If you only want to go between the two, it doesn't really matter how many potential destinations there are. So, any potential A to B trip through a network of arbitrary size is effectively just one direct route. The other points in the network might as well not exist.

Nevertheless, finding the most efficient way to move between a significant number of different destinations in a large network – known in combinatorics as "The Travelling Salesman Problem" – is so hard that computers cannot reliably manage the task.

WHY IS IT SO TOUGH?

ANSWER
PG/184

SCUDDER

In the American theocracy of the Second Revolution, any hint of disobedience to the whims of the Prophet Incarnate is punished ruthlessly. Despite his public piety, and his brutal enforcement of dogma and morality, the Prophet is a cruel, sinful man, opposed by a small seditious group who call themselves the Cabal.

The Springford Prayer Station is a lonely, sprawling countryside chapel, out of the way and in poor repair. Cabal member John Lyle arrives there one evening, half an hour after the afternoon's rain has finally eased off, so that he can check it out as a possible useful location. The Cabal always needs quiet but plausible destinations – the quieter the better, as the Prophet's forces know all too well. It's a dangerous dance they engage in.

The prayer station's rutted car park is a minefield of deep puddles, so he is careful to park next to another car's dry spot. From the outside, the station is an unprepossessing place, stark and utilitarian, in need of a fresh coat of whitewash. It's a little better inside, clean and tidy, the benches polished and the altar shining. The custodian is an avuncular older man, neatly presented, with a warm smile and kind eyes. He nods to John as he enters, but makes no effort to intrude, staying at his place inside the door. John takes a place near the altar, out of the custodian's sight, and sits quietly for a while, feigning prayer.

When he leaves, he asks the custodian if it's been a busy day, and the man ruefully informs him that he's the first visitor since noon. John thanks him and leaves.

ONCE HE'S SAFELY BACK IN HIS CAR AND ON THE ROAD, HE CROSSES THE STATION OFF HIS MENTAL LIST OF POSSIBLE VENUES. WHY?

ANSWER
PG/185

CAPTIVITY

David MacKinnon is a dreamer and idealist in a utopian society where mental issues can be technologically repaired. Having been arrested for assault, he is assessed as being a danger for violent offences in the future. He is offered a choice – accept cure, or be exiled to Coventry, the walled-off region of Earth where those who refuse the social norms are sent to live.

Fearing the boredom of normal society, he chooses exile, only to discover that rather than the easy-going anarchy he'd hoped for, Coventry is a collection of violent, brutally oppressive nations, one a dictatorship, one a religious state and one a corrupt faux-democracy. He is jailed as soon as he arrives, and everything he possesses is stripped from him.

While planning his escape, MacKinnon is faced with getting through a regularly patrolled room, which holds three doors. One will carry him onward, while the other two only lead to storerooms. He has no idea which is which. He doesn't have any keys, so the door locks need to be cut out, a process that will take him 10 minutes with the knife that he has been able to obtain. To make matters worse, one of the two storerooms contains a second security trigger, and opening its door will make bolts shoot across the other two doors, increasing the time it takes to then cut them open to 15 minutes.

GUARDS COME THROUGH THE ROOM EVERY 30 MINUTES. IF DAVID WAITS UNTIL THE GUARD HAS JUST LEFT, ARE THE ODDS OF ESCAPING BEFORE THE MAN RETURNS IN HIS FAVOUR?

ANSWER
PG/185

SERVICE

General Services is a company that has become incredibly successful through a very simple strategy – they will help you with any personal service whatsoever, provided it's not illegal. Whatever you need them for, whether it's creating a bespoke car or taking your dog for a walk, they'll take care of it. For a suitable price, of course.

Then a seemingly impossible request comes their way. A politically sensitive conference needs to host delegates from across the solar system, and they are hired to arrange it. The dilemma is that the conference absolutely needs to be held on the surface of Earth, but many of the delegates are unable to cope with the planet's comparatively high gravity.

ANSWER
PG/185

Earth's political leadership flatly refuses to permit the conference to take place anywhere else, not even in Earth orbit or at a human embassy off-planet. It must take place at ground level on the planet Earth. Cancelling the conference is inconceivable – it is a vital meeting – but the required location is physiologically impossible for many of the delegates. Telepresence and other forms of virtual attendance are likewise ruled out by the conference's sensitivity. The delegates have to meet in person.

WHAT IS GENERAL SERVICES' APPROACH TO SOLVING THE SEEMINGLY INSOLUBLE PROBLEM?

DETAILS

As part of a very drunk argument with a friend about whether the Venusian workforce is enslaved or not, an Earthman named Humphrey Wingate signs up to work on the planet. He doesn't remember what he's done until some time later, but it doesn't matter; the contract is fully binding, he's already there, and he owes a fortune to the company for his travel to the planet.

Wingate's debt is purchased by a struggling farmer, to be set off against his future earnings. He's free to leave, as soon as he has worked the debt off. In the meantime, he also needs food and water which, cashless, he has to buy on credit, along with a constant supply of a local herb called rhira that he needs to sleep.

Assume that Wingate owes $100,000, and that the interest on that debt is 1% per month. He notionally makes $200 a day, but after his daily deductions for tax, fees, rhira, housing, food and water, that's cut down to just $35.

IF HE PUTS EVERY CENT HE EARNS TOWARD HIS DEBT, HOW LONG, ROUGHLY, WILL IT TAKE HIM TO EARN HIS FREEDOM?

ANSWER
PG/186

SHUTTLE

Captain Jake Pemberton is a space pilot on the regular run between Supra-New York and the Moon's Space Terminal. During one particularly trying trip, a disruptive child manages to set off the hull breach alarm, causing widespread panic. Pemberton verifies that it's not a real problem, and eventually manages to calm the passengers down again. During the chaos, however, a diplomatic courier's documents are stolen from their locker on the upper service deck. Despite the chaos, only three people could possibly have had the opportunity. He speaks to each of them briefly about whether they saw anything suspicious in the area of the lockers, pretending that he is trying to discover who was responsible for setting off the alarm.

Alan is the ship's purser. "I was up there when the alarm went off, yes. When I realized how much chaos the alarm had caused, I went down to the main deck to help keep people calm. If the prankster was near the lockers, he waited until I was gone before joining the chaos. When I got back upstairs, everything looked like it had before."

Michael is a passenger. "I was up here during the false alarm, yes. Maybe I'm fatalistic, but there didn't seem much point in panicking. I decided to finish my drink and my newspaper like a civilized person. If anyone opened one of the lockers, I didn't see them, but my attention was on the sports pages."

Donald is the upper service deck's bartender. "Lockers? No. No, I just told you, I didn't see a damn thing. If you must know, I was sitting on the floor, so my view was completely blocked. Yes, behind the bar. Why do you think? We've got an emergency oxygen canister down there in case a customer has breathing trouble. No, I didn't need to open it, so don't even dream of deducting it from my wages."

WHO IS THE THIEF?

ANSWER
PG/188

SUNLIGHT

Bill is a crewman on a spaceship travelling between Earth and Mars, and when the communications antenna develops a fault, he is picked to go outside and repair it. The task is a hazardous one, because the ship is spinning in order to generate internal artificial gravity.

The ship's crewed portion, which the antenna is attached to, is a cylinder 200m across. In order to generate an Earth-like 1g of gravity at the surface, the ship rotates at 3rpm. Therefore, as Bill is crawling along the outside of the ship on the way to the antenna, his tangential velocity – the speed he'd fly away at if he fell off the ship's surface – is 31.4 metres per second, or a little over 70 miles per hour.

THE ANTENNA IS 150M LONG, BUT BILL ONLY HAS TO CLIMB OUT A QUARTER OF THAT WAY TO GET TO ITS PANEL, SO HE CAN CORRECT THE FAULT. WHEN BILL LOSES HIS GRIP TRYING TO CLOSE THE PANEL AGAIN, HOW QUICKLY IS HE MOVING AWAY FROM THE SHIP?

ANSWER PG/188

GOVERNOR

As mentioned elsewhere, Ira Howard was a philanthropist who became very rich in the USA after the Civil War, thanks to clever management and investment during the Reconstruction. He left his fortunes in trust to a foundation, whose task was to lengthen the human lifespan. Its administrators brought members of extremely long-lived families together and provided financial incentives to intermarry. Shrewd investments during the Great Depression – aided by knowledge provided by a time-travelling Family member – made the Howard Foundation and the Families extremely wealthy. In time, the 18 Howard Families developed lifespans of several centuries.

As the Families became ever more closely intertwined, the matter of ancestry and relationship got steadily more byzantine. Let us assume that Bob Rumsey, now in his fourteenth decade, decides to spend a pleasant afternoon in the company of his father's brother-in-law, his brother's father-in-law, his father-in-law's brother, and his brother-in-law's father.

WHAT IS THE MINIMUM POSSIBLE NUMBER OF INDIVIDUALS THAT THIS MIGHT INVOLVE?

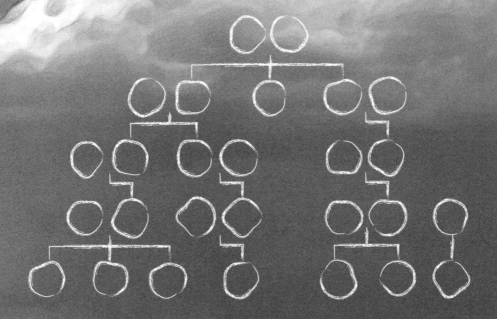

ANSWER
PG/189

VACUUM

During a visit to the Moon, Earth reporter Jack Arnold goes to an observatory to get a tour of their facility expansion project in the hope of getting an extra story. Knowles, the financial officer, agrees to show him around, although there's not all that much to see. Arnold is dismayed to learn that the Moon suffers from occasional quakes, caused by the same tidal forces that make the sea level rise and fall.

Knowles and Arnold are in an empty tunnel section talking to one of the engineers, Konski, when the tunnel is hit by a crashing mail rocket. The debris pokes a two-inch hole in the tunnel wall, down near floor level, and the men rapidly start losing their air.

Although Konski has on a suit of protective material, it doesn't have its own air supply, and Knowles and Arnold are even worse off, just wearing normal clothes. The leak will empty the tunnel of air in a matter of minutes, too swiftly for either escape or rescue to be possible. None of the men are carrying anything that might prove useful for sealing the leak, there's nothing in the tunnel with them, and the automatic sealant systems are unable to deal with such a hole of that size.

HOW DO THEY BUY TIME?

ANSWER
PG/189

HEINLEIN

HOW MUCH DO YOU KNOW ABOUT ROBERT A HEINLEIN AND HIS WORKS?

A. Which of the following sci-fi neologisms did Heinlein coin?
i. Frak.
ii. Grok.
iii. Grud.
iv. Smeg.

B. Heinlein is typically regarded as having invented which of the following?
i. Mobile phone.
ii. Hovercraft.
iii. Mecha.
iv. Waterbed.

C. Which branch of the military did Heinlein serve in?
i. Air Force.
ii. Army.
iii. Marines.
iv. Navy.

D. After writing, what was Heinlein's favourite solo pastime?
i. Blacksmithing.
ii. Clay sculpting.
iii. Stonemasonry.
iv. Woodcarving.

E. What was Heinlein's middle name?
i. Alder.
ii. Anson.
iii. Asher.
iv. Avery.

ANSWER
PG/189

F. Which of these movies was not associated with Heinlein's work?
i. *Predestination.*　　**ii.** *The Puppet Masters.*
iii. *Starship Troopers.*　　**iv.** *Total Recall.*

G. In the novel of the same title, Friday refers to:
i. An artificial person.　　**ii.** An executive assistant.
iii. A spaceship.　　**iv.** A weekday.

H. According to the title of Heinlein's novel, *The Moon is...* what?
i. A Balloon.　　**ii.** A Harsh Mistress.
iii. On Fire.　　**iv.** All Tomorrow's Parties.

I. What was Heinlein's name for his projected timeline of humanity?
i. Future History.　　**ii.** Technic History.
iii. Hainish Cycle.　　**iv.** Third Millennium.

J. In the novel of the same name, what was *The Number of the Beast* actually enumerating?
i. Alternate dimensions.　　**ii.** Demons.
iii. Worlds.　　**iv.** Howard Family members.

ARTHUR C CLARKE

1917 - 2008

CLARKE'S
BIOGRAPHY

THE THIRD MEMBER OF THE "BIG THREE", ARTHUR C CLARKE WAS A SCIENTIST AND FUTURIST, AS WELL AS ONE OF THE MOST SUCCESSFUL SCIENCE-FICTION WRITERS OF ALL TIME. HE WON MULTIPLE HUGO AND NEBULA AWARDS FOR HIS WRITING, AND AS ONE OF THE FIRST GREAT GAY SCIENCE-FICTION WRITERS HE BROUGHT A MORE DIVERSE OUTLOOK TO THE GENRE. HE WAS ALSO COMMEMORATED WITH THE UNESCO KALINGA PRIZE FOR HIS EXCEPTIONAL SKILLS AT PRESENTING DIFFICULT SCIENTIFIC IDEAS CLEARLY TO THE GENERAL POPULACE.

Born in England, Clarke made Sri Lanka his home for over 50 years of his life. It was there that he penned the majority of his greatest works — and also where he explored the seas as a scuba diver, discovering an ancient underwater ruined temple at Trincomalee, for example. However, it was space exploration, not deep-sea diving, that made his name.

The "Space Odyssey" series is one of the best known to those less familiar with the science-fiction genre, helped in no small part by the haunting movie *2001: A Space Odyssey*, on which Stanley Kubrick and Clarke collaborated. They worked together so closely on the project, in fact, that the movie was actually released in advance of the novel. This novel was just one of many stories in which Clarke explored a major theme of his works: the issue of first contact with aliens, and the evolutionary and technological leaps that could result from it.

ARTHUR C CLARKE'S SELECTED SCIENCE-FICTION BIBLIOGRAPHY

A Space Odyssey Series

2001: A Space Odyssey

2010: Odyssey Two

2061: Odyssey Three

3001: The Final Odyssey

Rama Series

Rendezvous with Rama

Rama II

The Garden of Rama

Rama Revealed

A Time Odyssey Series

Time's Eye

Sunstorm

Firstborn

Select Other Novels

Against the Fall of the Night

Childhood's End

The City and the Stars

A Fall of Moondust

Imperial Earth

The Fountains of Paradise

The Songs of Distant Earth

The Hammer of God

The Light of Other Days

Select Short Story Collections

The Sentinel

CRISES

Dr Wilson is a selenologist specializing in lunar geology, and in the far-flung future of 1996, he and his team are investigating the spectacular *Mare Crisium*, or Sea of Crises. It's a huge plain 300 miles across, surrounded by mountains, and previously unexplored. As expected, the plain is meteor-scarred, and coated with a thick layer of the cosmic dust that builds up on every astronomical body that doesn't have any protective atmosphere.

On one of the peaks surrounding the *Mare Crisium*, Dr Wilson discovers a clearly artificial device – a polished pyramid of a mineral of uncertain nature. This alone would be fascinating, but the pyramid and the ground immediately around it are free of dust and meteor damage. This turns out to be because of a spherical force field surrounding the device. Later analysis discovers that it is transmitting a simple signal off into deep space.

After years of investigation, other teams of scientists eventually manage to breach the force field. Although the device ought to be unharmed by the breach, it stops transmitting immediately. In fact, the device is indeed unharmed, and the force field's absence does not interfere with the device's function in any way.

SO WHY DOES THE SIGNAL STOP?

ANSWER
PG/190

CRITTERS

Robert Armstrong is making his way across a small, barren world from his base camp to the spaceport at Port Sanderson. His aim is to be there in time to catch the monthly ship off the planetoid and head back toward civilization. It's an inhospitable place on the edge of the galaxy, close to its little red sun, with no useful atmosphere and not a trace of water or vegetation. During the day, the solar radiation is as potent as the cold is during the night. No non-human life has ever been observed on it.

En route, his transport breaks down, and he is forced to resort to walking through the darkness. He has time to make it to his ship, provided he doesn't dawdle. Even when his torch fails, he's resolved to keep going.

Long-term residents of Port Sanderson talk in hushed tones about a monster in the darkness, and one man insists he heard it following him on a similar walk into the port. Armstrong is far too scientific to be worried by ghost stories, however. The planetoid is barren – no air, no water, no soil, no geothermal energy, nothing that might help life develop – and so he has to be safe.

WHAT HAS HE FORGOTTEN?

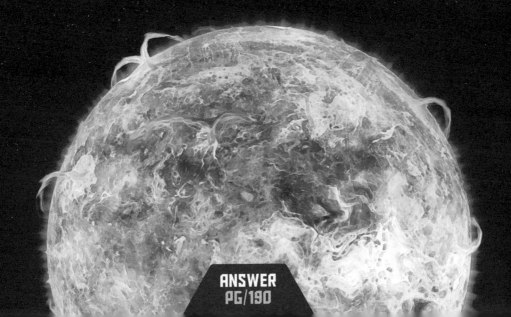

ANSWER
PG/190

MALICE

It's the early 1960s. While diving for pearls off the coast of Queensland, Australia, Szabo Tibor sees a lunar capsule crash into the sea near his boat, its chute tangled. He rushes over to where it is and sees that the capsule is Russian. The cosmonaut is too hurt to talk but is able to knock in response to Tibor's questions and comments. It transpires that the capsule is damaged and the door will not open. The inhabitant is running out of air.

After the annexation of Hungary by the Russians, and the murder of his brother by a Russian soldier, Tibor is eager for a chance for some revenge. He taunts the cosmonaut about their situation and informs them that he is going to ensure their death. He then sets about greatly delaying the Australian rescue efforts. By the time he takes the rescuers to the capsule, the cosmonaut has long since run out of air, and is dead.

WHEN THE CAPSULE IS OPENED, THE RESCUERS DISCOVER DEFINITIVE PROOF THAT TIBOR DELIBERATELY MURDERED THE COSMONAUT. HOW IS THIS POSSIBLE?

ANSWER
PG/191

DEUS

According to the teachings of one small, strange sect of Tibetan Buddhist monks, the purpose of the Universe is to list all of the approximately nine billion names of God. Once this task is complete, existence will cease, its purpose fulfilled. The sect works to fulfil God's design, listing all the names. In the divine alphabet used for the purpose, each of God's names is nine characters long.

It's a task that they expect will take more than 15,000 years, but when computer technology starts becoming available, they are quick to make use of this new tool. They purchase and install a huge American computer and set it to outputting the names of God on printer paper.

NOW, SOME OF THE POSSIBLE COMBINATIONS OF THE LETTERS ARE NOT VALID NAMES. IN FACT, A LITTLE UNDER HALF OF THE POSSIBLE COMBINATIONS ARE NOT ACTUALLY NAMES OF GOD. HOW MANY LETTERS ARE THERE IN THAT ALPHABET?

ANSWER
PG/191

ZEUS

After the explosive destruction of Jupiter and its transformation into a new sun, its former moons are transformed into a small new star system nestled within the solar system. The unknown aliens responsible for the procedure have a particular interest in Europa, which is now a cloud-draped planet with extensive oceans and a breathable oxygen atmosphere. Human presence on Europa is strictly forbidden, and lethally enforced, even though the aliens themselves are thought to be 900 light years away. Ganymede is now perfectly suited for human life, however, and colonization efforts are under way.

Europa's clouds hide many tantalizing mysteries, but among them all one of the most enigmatic is Mount Zeus, a vast mountain that appeared on the new planet after Jupiter's transformation. There was no hint of it before, and no amount of upheaval could have generated sufficient volcanic activity to account for Mount Zeus's presence.

WHAT CREATED IT?

ANSWER
PG/192

SKYBIKE

Rama is the name given to a huge cylindrical spaceship of alien origin that is observed passing through the solar system. The human crew sent out to investigate the ship discover that it contains an artificial habitat – a landscaped space that wraps around the inside of the cylinder, which is around 30 miles long and 60 miles in diameter. It includes apparent countryside, towns and cities, road networks and even a sea. The air is safely breathable, the atmosphere similar in density to Earth's and, because *Rama* is spinning, the habitat has artificial gravity – albeit lighter than Earth's. What the ship does not appear to contain is any intelligent life.

One of the exploration team, Jimmy, smuggles a skybike onto the ship, and heads off joyriding. When he gets close to the back end of the ship, a discharge from the engine systems crashes his bike, and he's stuck up in the mountains at that end of the ship, at the top of a 1,500ft cliff. He's prevented from trying to repair his bike when a crab-like critter chops it into pieces and dumps the bits into a pit, apparently clearing up. It ignores Jimmy completely.

There's no other skybike available, or any other source of flight, so he has to find some way to get down the cliff so that his colleagues can rescue him. The gravity is light, but calculations show that it's not quite light enough for him to just leap off and survive the fall. The cliff is too sheer to safely attempt climbing, and there's no way to contrive enough rope, a harness or other necessary tools. The exploration team, who have no intention of going up into the mountains, have no equipment that might be useful.

HOW DOES JIMMY GET DOWN SAFELY?

ANSWER
PG/192

MALFUNCTION

Astronauts David Bowman and Frank Poole are on the spaceship *Discovery One*, heading to Saturn's moon, Iapetus. The ship's sentient computer, HAL 9000, or just "Hal", is in charge of running the *Discovery*, as well as obtaining and relaying accurate information during the mission's tests and analyses.

Cognitive research has discovered that all humans have an inbuilt xenophobic reaction to alien life and technology. To avoid contaminating the experiments that the crew have to perform, and to keep them psychologically safe, only Hal is informed that the real mission is to investigate a theorized alien presence on Iapetus. The human scientists know the broad outline of the mission, but their knowledge of alien involvement is kept strictly suppressed.

Over time, Hal starts to become erratic. Bowman and Poole discuss the matter with mission control on Earth, and are ordered to take the computer offline so that the problem can be identified and corrected. Hearing this, Hal severs all lines of communication with Earth. It uses a space exploration pod to kill Poole and voids the internal atmosphere to try to kill Bowman.

IT LATER TRANSPIRES THAT THERE IS NOTHING WRONG WITH HAL ITSELF. ITS HARDWARE AND SOFTWARE WERE PERFORMING AS DESIGNED. SO WHY DID IT MALFUNCTION?

ANSWER
PG/192

BUNKHOUSE

During the construction of a space station out beyond the Moon, the inhabitants of Bunkhouse Six are horrified when a wrenching jolt wakes them up in the middle of their sleep cycle. Getting out of bed, they quickly discover the truth – the absence of artificial gravity means that the bunkhouse has come loose from the rim of the rotation station, and is floating off into space.

While a rescue craft is able to arrive before the men run out of air, there is an issue – there are no spacesuits or pressure locks inside the bunkhouse, because it's supposed to be a fixed part of the station habitat. The rescuers can open the bunkhouse up, but there's no pressurized tunnel or anything. The men will have to spend a period of time – up to 20 seconds – in a vacuum, most of it completely open to space, as they are pushed over and into the craft's airlock.

There's no option, however. It's that or run out of air inside the bunkhouse, so they go ahead.

WHAT INJURIES DO THEY SUFFER?

ANSWER
PG/193

CRUISE

Pat Harris is the captain of the *Selene*, a dust-cruiser that takes lunar tourists on a trip across the *Mare Sitium*, or Sea of Thirst, on the Moon. This area is a vast patch of super-fine rock dust, perfectly dry, so delicately grained that it behaves like water. During one trip, a moonquake collapses a cavern beneath the *Selene*. The ship sinks almost 50 feet into the dust, becoming trapped.

Although the dust doesn't present any danger of crushing the cruiser, which is sturdy, there are a number of deadly issues for the crew to deal with. The cruiser is unable to broadcast a signal to the lunar base and, since the trips aren't actively tracked, rescuers will not be certain precisely where the cruiser was when it sank. Therefore they have no idea how long they have to survive. Air is a primary concern, of course. Water and food can last until long after the air has run out. Another issue is the slow but relentless seeping of dust into the damaged cruiser, which is eroding the available space. There are no hostile creatures, at least, and Captain Harris and his crew are able to prevent dangerous levels of panic and aggression.

CAN YOU THINK OF ANOTHER PRESSING ISSUE THAT THREATENS THE LIVES OF EVERYONE ON BOARD?

ANSWER
PG/193

INVERTED

When a superconductive power plant is briefly overloaded, engineer Richard Nelson is caught in a set of unprecedented power fluctuations. After he comes round, he is baffled by the fact that all the text he can see looks backwards. Furthermore, his wedding ring, which he is unable to remove from his finger, is on the other hand. A bemused medical examination confirms the truth – Nelson has been laterally inverted, on a molecular level. Even the writing in his diary and the coins in his pocket have been inverted, as if being plucked, whole, from the reflection of a mirror.

Scientists puzzling over Nelson's problem eventually realize that he has to have been rotated in a fourth dimension, one beyond the perceptible confines of physical space. After a time, they further realize that, to turn him back, they are going to have to attempt another inversion. They don't have much time, because Nelson is starting to starve.

WHY?

ANSWER
PG/194

FLYBOY

Despite being only 16, Roy Malcolm is such an expert in aviation history that he is able to win a national competition held by World Airways, Inc. His prize is a trip on the rocket ship *Sirius* to Inner Station, a spaceport five hundred miles above Earth. Up on the station, he befriends some of the younger apprentices, and the group quickly become as thick as thieves.

When the spaceship *Cygnus* arrives, the secretive nature of the crew quickly arouses the boys' suspicions of piracy and other villainy. Following the well-loved televisual example of Dan Drummond, Space Detective, they decide to investigate. The *Cygnus* is a forbidding vessel, and attempts to get the crew to talk are spectacular failures. Eventually, they catch the ship unattended and sneak on board to have a look around. They're horrified to discover that the vessel is holding several highly advanced ray guns, far beyond anything known to society, as well as aggressive-looking armoured spacesuits and a number of other dangerous-looking hand-to-hand weapons.

Carrying objects to Inner Station is still expensive, so nothing is on board the *Cygnus* frivolously or accidentally. The guns and other suspicious items are not for delivery, nor are they for display, collection or self-defence.

DESPITE THE SECRECY OF THE CREW, HOWEVER, THEY ARE THERE FOR A PERFECTLY INNOCENT PURPOSE. CAN YOU THINK WHAT?

ANSWER
PG/194

SECRETS

Henry Cooper is a scientific reporter with a speciality in maths. Heading back to the Moon on behalf of the United Nations Space Agency in order to write some more favourable articles, he finds his friends there unusually distant and reticent. He becomes curious and, after some digging around, the police commissioner relents and takes him to an obscure lab. There, the head scientist explains that they've discovered a technique that would prevent people dying from old age until they're at least two hundred years old. This, however, he considers to be a disaster.

The world is already overcrowded – six billion people crammed together, using more resources each year than the planet can provide. The seas have already been turned into farming space, so that land can be used for homes and businesses, and this is with an average life expectancy of only 84 years. He's terrified that, if news gets out and the technique goes mainstream, the global population will immediately spiral to 14 billion or more.

ASSUMING THAT SUCH A POPULATION WOULD, INDEED, CRASH SOCIETY, ARE HIS FEARS WELL FOUNDED?

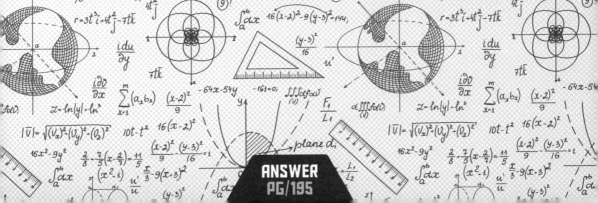

ANSWER
PG/195

EARLY

The Russian spaceship *Leonov* has travelled to the orbit of Jupiter as part of an ongoing joint USA-USSR effort to investigate the deaths aboard the American spaceship *Discovery One*. Additionally, there are anomalous events occurring within Jupiter's atmosphere, and the *Discovery*'s original mission seems to bear these out. Tensions between the two great nations are high, but without intervention the *Discovery* will burn up in Jupiter's atmosphere. Only the *Leonov* is able to reach it in time.

The *Leonov* reaches the *Discovery* on schedule. With weeks to go until the return launch window, there is more than enough time for a full investigation. This will give the team plenty of opportunity to investigate why HAL, the *Discovery*'s on-board AI, malfunctioned so

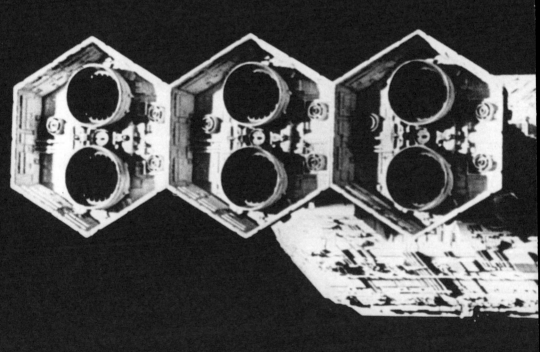

ANSWER
PG/196

lethally. Even when escalating international tensions force the two crews into segregation on their own nations' crafts, no particular danger is evident. The two ships will just return separately.

However, as Jupiter is swiftly devoured by a self-replicating alien device, it becomes clear that if the teams do not leave the planet's orbit immediately, they will all die. However, if they do leave separately before the launch window, they will not be able to return to Earth.

WHY MIGHT THIS BE?

NORTH

Secret agent K-15 is forced to go to ground on Phobos, one of the moons of Mars. He has been pursued there by the space-cruiser *Doradus*. His own government have help on the way – a much larger and more dangerous ship than the *Doradus* – but they are a while out. Although Phobos is larger than Deimos, the other Martian moon, it's still small, with an equator of less than 45 miles in length. It is also quite light for its size, so its gravity is quite minimal – just 1/2000th of Earth's – and there's no atmosphere.

The *Doradus* is a human-piloted pursuit vessel capable of high speeds, and it has an impressive battery of front-facing pinpoint lasers – they won't harm the moon, but they'll slice through agent K-15 instantly. It's also very fast, with a base forward acceleration of 1,000 metres per second squared, a top speed of 1,500,000 miles per hour, and manoeuvring thrusters in the other orthogonal directions that are only 50% less powerful.

K-15, on the other hand, may be clever but he is significantly slower than normal – without much gravity to offer good friction to the surface of Deimos, he can only manage one mile an hour running. He can get up to 30mph if he launches himself into a well-braced jump, but then, of course, he's unable to change course until he lands again, a couple of minutes later.

IF K-15 CAN SOMEHOW SURVIVE THREE HOURS, THE *DORADUS* WILL HAVE TO RETREAT, AND HE WILL BE SAFE. DO YOU FANCY HIS CHANCES?

ANSWER
PG/197

VIRAL

US astronaut Frank Poole, part of the crew of *Discovery One*, was killed when its sentient computer, HAL, flung him out into deep space. A thousand years later, in the year 3001, his body is recovered by a comet-gathering tug, and he is revived using new technology. Some decades later, he is contacted from the planet Europa by Halman, a disembodied sentience that is the fusion of HAL with his old colleague, Dave Bowman.

Halman exists inside the monolith that stands on Europa's surface, and explains to Poole that this enigmatic object is part of a network constructed and run by the highly advanced residents of a planet 450 light years away. When Jupiter was ignited a thousand years ago, the monolith broadcast a message back toward its home and, after a century of consideration on the part of the aliens, the reply has now arrived. The monolith is ordered to wipe out humanity for being an over-aggressive, failed species.

With Halman's help, Poole sabotages the local monolith so that the attempt to blot out the Sun fails. Unfortunately, there is no way to stop the failure being reported, and Halman is certain that the aliens will attempt some more direct way to destroy humankind. Poole agrees, but is not unduly worried.

WHY NOT?

ANSWER
PG/198

WEAPON

Some time before the Battle of the Five Suns, Professor-General Malavar decided that it was important for the Combined Research Staff to ascertain as precisely as possible the point at which pain became impossible for a person to endure.

In return for a significant amount of money, Malavar connected fully-informed volunteers to a finely tuneable pain crystal. They were subjected to shocks of pain of increasing intensity via the crystal, and then given some time to recover. However, each increase in pain was just low enough that the volunteer was unable to differentiate it from the one before. Each time the pain level increased, the amount of money the volunteer earned also increased, but substantially so rather than infinitesimally. This ensured that all the volunteers were strongly motivated to endure as far as possible.

Unfortunately, this methodology threw up an issue. Put yourself in the place of one of the volunteers. There is, obviously, a level of pain that you are not prepared to endure. You want to stop just before that. But it's impossible to tell the difference from one jolt to the next. If the next shock is too much, the previous one would have been as well, so you need to have stopped before it. But, conversely, if the pain you felt last time was acceptable, then the next one will also feel acceptable, and it will make you a lot richer.

WHEN DO YOU STOP?

ANSWER
PG/198

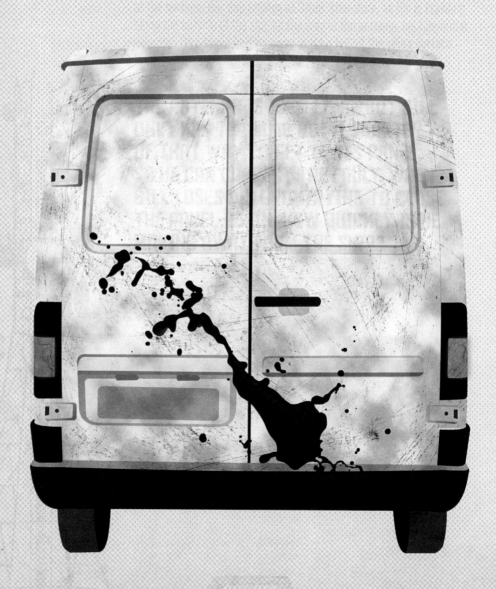

HARRY

Harry Purvis was based near the government's super-secret Atomic Energy Research Establishment (AERE) laboratories, outside the small village of Clobham. Word in the village was that the lab was working on some very dangerous, futuristic technology. He was in the pub one afternoon with some other regulars when a suspiciously anonymous truck careened down the hill from the direction of the AERE, smashing through a hedge into the field on the other side, where it overturned.

As the regulars looked down on the scene, a pair of white-overalled men staggered out of the van, took one look at the open back, and ran off at a dead sprint. Harry decided to investigate.

As he approached the crash site, his first thought was that some sort of liquid had been spilled. The back of the van, and the ground around it, appeared to be a mess of broken crates, which were covered with a thick black fluid. This substance appeared to be roiling and seething, which was bad, but nowhere near as bad as the way that it seemed to be defying gravity. A thick smear of it inched up the back of the van and then wavered away from the metal to flail around slowly in the air like some horrible pseudopod, shrinking and growing. He became aware of a noise then; a sinister, throbbing thrum, low and angry. Other parts of the patch also lifted, holding themselves off the ground before sinking back into the mass.

HARRY STOOD HIS GROUND RESOLUTELY AND EVENTUALLY REALIZED WHAT HE WAS LOOKING AT. IT DIDN'T INVOLVE MODERN TECHNOLOGY, LET ALONE FUTURISTIC RUMOURED TECH. WHAT WAS IT?

ANSWER
PG/198

CACTUS

Professor Surov was found dead on the surface of the Moon, shot precisely through the eye and left crumpled next to his new creation – a ripe, living plant able to thrive on the Moon's surface. Surov's Cactus, as it became known, was not, in fact, a cactus, but an entirely new engineered organism. Thick, leathery skin allowed it to survive in a vacuum and weather both the heat and cold of the lunar environment. Reproduction was via seeds, which were about the size of a plum kernel, although significantly more massive. Its roots were highly acidic, allowing it to penetrate and cling to the rocky surface, as well as to dissolve the feldspars and other minerals it needed to extract oxygen and other nutrients. Because of the absence of winds to float upon, the seeds were designed to take advantage of the low gravity and eject out hundreds of yards. It was, quite simply, a triumph, and in a surprisingly short time, the Cactus had colonized huge swathes of the Moon's surface.

Surov's research was brilliant, but not controversial. He had no enemies, professional or personal. No one wanted him to fail. The lunar colony at the time was purely scientific, and no one had desperate secrets to hide. Everyone in the colony was sane, functional and busy with their own work. In those early days of space, there were no space pirates or bandits, no aliens, no colonies on other planets. Security-force presence was minimal because it wasn't needed. No one wanted Surov dead at all, and he certainly didn't take his own life.

SO WHY WAS HE SHOT?

ANSWER
PG/199

PERFECT

The discovery of the asteroid that would become known as Richardson-115 caused something of a sensation, because initial observations suggested that it was unusually close to being spherical. As interest grew, increasingly powerful observatories were brought into the fray, and the large asteroid's apparent perfection grew more baffling. Finally, a manned ship was sent to investigate. Close assessment confirmed what everyone but the staunchest sceptics now suspected – Richardson-115 was a perfect sphere down to the nanometre level, without any hint of blemish or impact scar whatsoever. It was just drifting, perfect, not tumbling, through the solar system.

When an exploration team were sent to the surface, they discovered that, while the material the asteroid was made from looked like rock, it was far harder than even diamond. Impossibly so, in fact. The artefactual nature of the asteroid was confirmed when the surface rippled, swallowed the team, and spat them out into the asteroid's hollow centre. Instruments quickly revealed that the inside was just as perfect a sphere as the outside, the walls a uniform thickness of a little less than one hundred feet.

The material of Richardson-115 was also significantly dense – enough that its impact on other nearby bodies had suggested it was unusually heavy when it was assumed to be solid.

WITH THAT IN MIND, WHAT SORT OF GRAVITATIONAL FORCES WOULD THE ASTEROID HAVE EXERTED ON THE EXPLORATION TEAM WHILE THEY WERE INSIDE?

ANSWER
PG/199

CLARKE

HOW MUCH DO YOU KNOW ABOUT ARTHUR C CLARKE AND HIS WORKS?

A. What was Clarke's nationality?
i. American.
ii. British.
iii. Canadian.
iv. South African.

b. Clarke's best-known work is the hugely influential movie *2001: A Space Odyssey*. Who directed it?
i. David Cronenberg.
ii. Alfred Hitchcock.
iii. Stanley Kubrick.
iv. Steven Spielberg.

C. In which branch of the military did Clarke serve during the Second World War?
i. Air force.
ii. Army.
iii. Marines.
iv. Navy.

D. The monolith from *2001: A Space Odyssey* and related works had very specific proportions to its dimensions. What were they?
i. 1:2:3.
ii. 1:3:6.
iii. 1:4:9.
iv. 1:5:12.

E. Which of the following water sports was Clarke an enthusiast of?
i. Scuba diving.
ii. Water skiing.
iii. Snorkelling.
iv. Swimming.

ANSWER
PG/199

F. Which of Clarke's Laws states that "Any sufficiently advanced technology is indistinguishable from magic"?
i. Zeroth.　　　　**ii.** First.
iii. Second.　　　**iv.** Third.

G. Which of the following long-term diseases did Clarke suffer from?
i. Glandular fever.　　**ii.** Guinea-worm disease.
iii. Malaria.　　　　　**iv.** Polio.

H. Clarke lived the majority of his long life in which country?
i. Cambodia.　　　**ii.** Sri Lanka.
iii. Thailand.　　　**iv.** Vietnam.

I. Which of the following was not a television show?
i. *Arthur C. Clarke's Mysterious Universe.*
ii. *Arthur C. Clarke's Mysterious World.*
iii. *Arthur C. Clarke's Strange World.*
iv. *Arthur C. Clarke's World of Strange Powers.*

J. A number of Clarke's stories are set in which fictional London pub?
i. The King's Head.　　**ii.** The Hare and Hounds.
iii. The Raven.　　　　**iv.** The White Hart.

URSULA K LE GUIN

1929 - 2018

BIOGRAPHY

IN WHAT HAD TRADITIONALLY BEEN AN UNFORTUNATELY MALE-DOMINATED GENRE, URSULA K LE GUIN WAS A FEMINIST TRAILBLAZER WITH HER MARVELLOUS SPECULATIVE FICTION. THE HAINISH CYCLE IS HER MOST COMPLETE SCIENCE-FICTION CREATION (HER CELEBRATED EARTHSEA SERIES FITS MORE INTO THE HIGH FANTASY TRADITION), AND IT WAS FOR *THE LEFT HAND OF DARKNESS* THAT SHE WON THE FIRST OF EIGHT HUGO AWARDS. IN DOING SO, SHE BECAME THE FIRST FEMALE WINNER OF THE HUGO AWARD FOR BEST NOVEL.

The Left Hand of Darkness takes place on a world inhabited by ambisexuals: creatures with no fixed sex. Le Guin's exploration of sex and gender – and particularly its effect on culture and society – was a theme throughout much of her work. Great enjoyment comes from her exploration of strange peoples and invented cultures, and it is no surprise that Le Guin's father was an anthropologist. It is a profession that occurs repeatedly throughout her writing.

Le Guin's writing is far less concerned with hard science than the "Big Three", but she often subverts classical tropes – whether regarding gender, morality, race or sexuality – in her writing in order to explore alternative societal and political structures. Consequently, she is regarded as not just one of the finest science-fiction writers, but one of the finest novelists of the twentieth century.

URSULA K LE GUIN'S SELECTED BIBLIOGRAPHY

Earthsea Series

A Wizard of Earthsea

The Tombs of Atuan

The Farthest Shore

Tehanu

The Other Wind

Hainish Cycle

Rocannon's World

Planet of Exile

City of Illusions

The Left Hand of Darkness

The Dispossessed

The Word for World is Forest (Novella)

The Telling

Select Other Novels

The Lathe of Heaven

Always Coming Home

Select Short Story Collections

Tales from Earthsea

Four Ways to Forgiveness

The Birthday of the World and Other Stories

Searoad

Changing Planes

ANSIBLE

An ansible is a device that is able to communicate instantly with other ansibles, regardless of distance. The principle of simultaneity it works on requires one of the communicating devices to be located on a reasonably massive planet, but otherwise the only restriction is the low bandwidth. Instant communication across great distance is vital to maintaining any sort of large-scale space-faring civilization, so the ansible is utterly critical to advanced civilization.

By way of example, consider a theoretical spaceship with an escalating acceleration drive – exactly the sort of vessel where an ansible is required to maintain any sort of functional contact with anyone. The drive starts slowly from the moment of engagement, doubling the ship's speed in 30 seconds, but it swiftly picks up. It then doubles the ship's speed again, but in half the time, just 15 seconds. The process repeats indefinitely, with the ship doubling its speed again and again, each iteration requiring precisely half the time taken on the previous doubling. With this type of drive, the mass-energy equivalence barrier is circumvented, so speeds above light are perfectly possible.

IRRESPECTIVE OF THE STARTING SPEED, HOW FAR WOULD IT BE FROM ITS ORIGIN JUST ONE MINUTE AFTER ENGAGING THE DRIVE?

ANSWER
PG/200

BEQUEST

Semley is a young noblewoman in a quasi-feudal civilization on the second planet orbiting Fomalhaut. Despite her lofty station, she is not especially wealthy. Her family heirloom, lost for centuries, is a necklace reputed to be of incredible beauty, constructed originally by the Gdemiar, a dwarf-like people who live underground.

Soon after the planet is contacted by the "starlords" – that is, the League of All Worlds, a galaxy-spanning human civilization – word reaches her that her heirloom is in a museum on a planet 10 light years away. When she contacts the Gdemiar, they inform her that the League has provided them with an almost light-speed spaceship. They can send her in the ship to collect the necklace, and the journey will take her just "one long night" each way. They offer to do so freely, without cost or obligation, and to return her home safely once she's done.

Semley delightedly agrees, and indeed finds the journey swift and painless. When she arrives at the museum, the curators return her necklace, which is every bit as wondrous as family legends had told her. That evening, she makes the journey back to Fomalhaut but, on arrival, is filled with horror.

WHAT HAS SHE FAILED TO CONSIDER?

ANSWER
PG/200

EMBARGO

Gaverel Rocannon is an ethnologist for the League of All Worlds who becomes aware of the technologically primitive society on Fomalhaut II after meeting one of its members in a League museum. He fights to get the planet placed under embargo, so that the societies there are able to develop naturally, without undue interference from the League. Sensors will even be put in place in space around the planet, to ensure that the League's enemies do not try to interfere.

Once the embargo is in place, he is allowed to travel to Fomalhaut II for ethnological purposes, to learn about and document the societies. All League ethnologists understand and accept the personal dangers of life on low-tech worlds. It can be a dangerous job, but it's an important one, and risks to life, health and sanity are part of it. The native life of the world poses no threat to the League and, while there is conflict, disease and suffering within its societies, it is no worse than that on most embargoed primitive worlds. Even its viruses are of no particular concern.

NEVERTHELESS, SHORTLY AFTER ARRIVING ON FOMALHAUT II, ROCANNON DISCOVERS THAT PLACING THE PLANET UNDER EMBARGO WAS A MISTAKE. MOREOVER, IT IS ONE THAT HAS THE POTENTIAL TO THREATEN THE LEAGUE ITSELF. WHY?

ANSWER
PG/201

SHING

The man known as Falk has suffered a memory wipe and knows nothing of his past or culture. After several years of living with agrarian locals, he is taken to the Shing, the telepathic rulers of the Earth. In contrast to the rest of the planet's inhabitants, who live in scattered, violent rural tribes, the Shing are highly advanced. Their reverence for life is absolute – they do not kill under any circumstances, and consume only vegetables. In fact, they have bio-engineered many animal and bird species to be able to speak eloquently in their own self-defence against humans.

The Shing explain that Falk is a human-alien hybrid who arrived on Earth years before, when his expedition's spaceship crashed. Although he survived the crash intact, he was attacked by rebels to Shing rule, who erased his memory. The Shing themselves are fully human, and they rule Earth now because the League of All Worlds self-destructed some centuries before. They keep the peace on Earth through the pretence of an enemy presence on the planet that prevents the aggressive tribes from fighting against them, which they admit is not ideal, but it works.

They learned of Falk's origins from another survivor of the crash, a young man named Orry, who was a young child on the original expedition. Now they intend to undo Falk's memory wipe, restoring his original personality and memories.

Falk does not trust the Shing at all. In fact, he believes that they are manipulative aliens; pathological liars desperate to maintain despotic rule over Earth. The only information that Falk is confident of is that confirmed as true by Orry – that they are both human-alien hybrids from another planet, and that the machine they intend to use to undo his mind-wipe will, indeed, do just that.

BUT IF HIS EXISTENCE THREATENS THE SHING, WHY WOULD THEY HELP HIM? IT'S NOT AS IF HIS LIFE IS IN ANY DANGER WITHOUT THEIR TREATMENT.

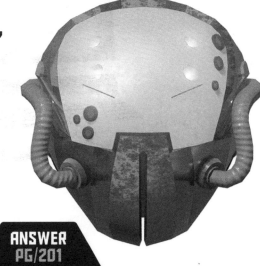

ANSWER
PG/201

FORETELLING

On the world of Gethen, certain adherents of the Handdarrate religion practise the art of foretelling, a seemingly precognitive talent that harnesses their intuition to provide reliable answers. They offer this service in return for a fee, as a way of teaching one of their core tenets.

When the Terran planetary recruiter Genly Ai asks if Gethen will have joined the coalition of human-settled worlds in five years, the answer is a simple yes, providing him with none of the guidance he might have hoped for regarding how to achieve such a thing.

For a practical example of your own, consider this question. There are four balls in a bag, identical apart from their colours. Two are red, one is white and one is blue. A person draws two balls from the bag at random, examines them, and informs you that at least one of them is red.

WHAT IS THE CHANCE THAT THE OTHER BALL SHE DREW IS ALSO RED?

ANSWER
PG/201

WALLS

Tau Ceti is home to two inhabited worlds: Urras and Annares. The latter is young – just two hundred years old – founded as an anarcho-syndicalist haven by unhappy rebels from Urras. Over the years, the Urrasti have come to consider Annares as almost a feudal mining serfdom of theirs, while the Annaresti consider themselves far freer than the Urrasti.

Shevek is an Annaresti physicist who finds himself on Urras for a time. He becomes deeply preoccupied with non-physical walls – not just the societal wall around him as an outsider, but the walls of privilege, the walls of physical possessions, the walls of social mores. He accuses the Urrasti of self-imposed imprisonment.

But self-imposed imprisonment need not be mental. Sit upright on a chair, so that your back is vertical, your thighs horizontal, and your lower legs vertical. Now, without leaning forward or moving your feet back, try to stand up.

WHY CAN'T YOU MOVE?

ANSWER
PG/202

FEAR

Having been recently discovered, World 4470 is the subject of an exploratory expedition from the League of All Worlds. It's temperate, with human-breathable atmosphere, plenty of water and reasonably calm weather patterns. The available landmass is covered with lush vegetation – vast prairies, heaths, forests, jungles – but there is no animal life whatsoever. All pollination is done by wind.

This suits the human sensor, Osden, just fine. An empath, he feels the emotions of the animals around him, people included, as if they were his own. With no way to turn this facility off, or isolate his genuine reactions from those he absorbs, he is always keen to get away from people.

As the team explore, something goes wrong. An empathic blanket of fear slowly grows around them, first affecting just Osden, but then getting strong enough to influence them all. It's definitely not being generated by the team. They wonder whether there is some sort of motile vegetable being – a plant monster with

ANSWER
PG/202

sufficient emotion to overwhelm them – and they uproot the camp, using the shuttle to relocate to a new site 12,000km away in a matter of a few hours. As soon as they land, however, they are met with the same overpowering fear they'd sought to escape.

Double-checking, they ensure that there is no animal life on World 4470. That includes the planet itself; it is not some sort of giant rock-monster planet. The trees and flowers and other plants they examine are all simple, and besides, the team is a vast distance from where they first landed. There are no out-of-phase creatures alongside them invisibly, no sentient gases, energy beings or other exotic, imperceptible life forms.

SO WHERE IS THE FEAR COMING FROM, AND HOW DID IT FOLLOW THEM ACROSS THE WORLD SO IMMEDIATELY?

YEARS

Laia is an influential anarchist philosopher nearing the end of her life. The turbulent years of her struggles and imprisonments are long past. The society she lives in is still quite oppressive, but her teachings have earned her a great deal of respect and attracted many adherents. Her home is within a commune founded on her principles, an Odonian House, and while she has passed on her torches, she remains an inspiring figure.

One particular day, out and about in her neighbourhood, Laia spends some time talking to a child, and reflects on being forced to grow up suddenly by harsh events. As part of this, she tells the child that she spent exactly an eighth of her life as a child, a fifth as a youth, a half as a woman, and, after her stroke, 14 years in decline.

HOW OLD IS LAIA?

ANSWER
PG/203

WILDER

Orrec Caspro is the heir to the domain of Caspromant, son of that territory's Brantor, Canoc. There are several domains, and each Brantor bloodline possesses a unique gift, which they use to protect their domain. The Caspro family possess the gift of unmaking – at a glance, they can will something or someone to destruction.

As Canoc's only child, Orrec is troubled by his inability to access the family gift as he approaches puberty. When it does arrive, however, he wishes it hadn't – it is completely outside his control. Although his father spends every waking moment attempting to train him in control, the gift quickly builds to the point where anything he looks at is destroyed. Horrified, Orrec blindfolds himself, giving up sight for good.

However, his mother takes ill and, as she is dying, she asks to see his eyes one last time. He reluctantly agrees and, to both their surprise, his regard does not destroy her. After her death, he risks a series of lone experiments, removing his blindfold alone, in a safe location, to try reading. Again, nothing untoward happens. As he gets bolder in his solitary tests, it becomes obvious that his gaze is as harmless as it ever was when he was a child. In fact, he can't even destroy something if he tries, even if he puts himself in identical situations to ones where he was destructive in the past.

HE DOESN'T FEEL ANY DIFFERENT AND, IN FACT, ABSOLUTELY NOTHING ABOUT HIS GIFT HAS CHANGED AT ANY POINT. GIVEN THAT CIRCUMSTANCES EXTERNAL TO ORREC DO NOT AFFECT HIS DESTRUCTIVE POWER IN ANY WAY, WHAT IS GOING ON?

ANSWER
PG/204

RESISTANCE

The ancient city of Ansul is dominated by the Alds, a repressive group who believe absolutely that writing is evil, and women are so inferior as to be beneath consideration, unfit for any purpose save child-bearing. They are not even allowed out on the streets. Memer is a young woman who lives in the house of Sulter, one of the secret sect of librarians who attempt to preserve the city's old knowledge and history.

Rebellion is brewing, and Memer becomes active in the network of women and men who seek to overthrow the Alds. At first, she is very scared, as the penalties for disobedience are horribly savage, but her friend Gry points out that, a lot of the time, she will be in far less danger than she thinks.

WHY IS THIS?

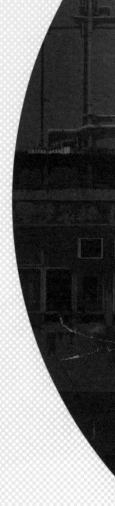

ANSWER
PG/204

GENERATIONAL

The *Discovery* is a generation ship, launched from Earth at sub-light speeds to spend centuries travelling in order to one day colonize a distant planet. The ship's population is kept strictly at 4,000 through contraceptives, and extensive protections are put in place to preserve the internal ecology from depletion, hoarding or disruption. All the scientific and technical knowledge that the future colonists will need to know on arrival is stored in the databanks, along with Earth's history, art and culture, as well as detailed explanations of why the planet's environment degraded.

As generations of new crew come and go, considerable misunderstanding and confusion builds regarding the zeroth generation, the people who set out in the *Discovery*. Even the idea of living on a planet seems strange. Tasks become ritualized as the understanding behind them fails. Interest in Earth's heritage fades away. The crew remember which instructions are important – what levers to pull and when – but not why.

PERHAPS THERE IS MEANING WITHOUT CONTEXT, AND PERHAPS NOT. CONSIDER THE FOLLOWING LIST OF OPTIONS, A TO D. IF YOU PICK ONE OF THEM ENTIRELY AT RANDOM, WHAT IS THE CHANCE THAT IT SHOWS THE PROBABILITY OF IT BEING THE CORRECT ANSWER TO THIS QUESTION?

A: 0%

B: 25%

C: 25%

D: 50%

ANSWER
PG/205

DRAGONS

The wizard of Sattins Island is a fat, bumbling man. True names are not used in Earthsea, but he is known as Underhill. He is not really very competent, but he is amiable enough, and not given to attempting to abuse his meagre powers. That suits the superstitious islanders just fine, until a black-bearded stranger arrives to see the wizard.

It turns out that Blackbeard is also a wizard, and he suspects Underhill of being in possession of a treasure stolen from his ancestors. The two battle, and when Blackbeard unleashes his opponent's true name, won at great cost, he inadvertently reveals Underhill's true form – the great black dragon Yevaud. Blackbeard is devoured on the spot, and Yevaud, forcibly reawakened to his predatory cruelty, goes on to ravage the island and its people.

Assume for now that the following statements related to dragons and their feeding habits are facts:

Every creature is suitable as food if it runs from danger.

When dragons are bored by a creature, they always ignore it.

No creatures taste good unless they are quick on their feet.

No deer fails to eat grass.

No creatures ever whine, except those in terror.

Hedgehogs are not suitable for food.

None but creatures that taste good eat grass.

Dragons are bored by creatures that whine.

The only creatures in terror are deer.

Creatures that are quick on their feet always run from danger.

DO DRAGONS EAT DEER?

ANSWER
PG/205

NAMING

In the language of creation, which is also the language of dragons, it is impossible for humans to lie – not because falsehood fails, but because the world itself shifts to ensure that what was spoken is true. This is the basis of all magic. Everything has a true name; the name that carries weight in the language of creation – each stone, each wave, each person. To know the true name of someone or something is to be able to speak about it in the language of creation. To take power over it.

Thus it is that names – true names – are the heart of magic. Wizards spend their entire lifetimes studying the true naming of things, and building the power required to speak sentences of creation. In a lifetime built of words, many echoes and synchronicities arise, and these can be vital conduits to revelation.

CONSIDER THE PAIR OF WORDS "NITROMAGNESITE" AND "REGIMENTATIONS". WHAT HIGHLY UNUSUAL TIE DO THEY SHARE?

ANSWER
PG/205

DRY

In their quest for immortality, the wizards of Earthsea accidentally created a hell for themselves, and all the other human inhabitants of the archipelago. The Dry Lands are dark, barren, void of purpose or emotion, and upon death the soul is trapped there. Caught. Outside the archipelago, the cycle of death and life progresses freely – death and rebirth – but within it eternal stagnation awaits.

On a chilly, mountainous island toward the archipelago's northern rim, a couple were found quietly dead in a high valley, lying hand in hand in a meadow of bright, new spring flowers. They were just a mile from the village where they lived. Whatever it was that killed them, it left no signs – there were no wounds, no broken bones, no bites or claws or stabs or bludgeons. Examination revealed no trace of poisons, diseases, magic or electrocution. Coincidence played no part in their joint death. They had not suffered simultaneous embolisms or strokes, and had certainly not committed suicide. No creature or monster had inflicted their deaths, not even something escaped from the Dry Lands. They had not even been robbed. With magic ruled out, it was certain that dragons and wizards were not to blame, turbulent though such beings were. Indeed, the cause of their death would be as familiar to an earthling as to an Archipelago islander.

HOW DID THEY DIE?

ANSWER
PG/206

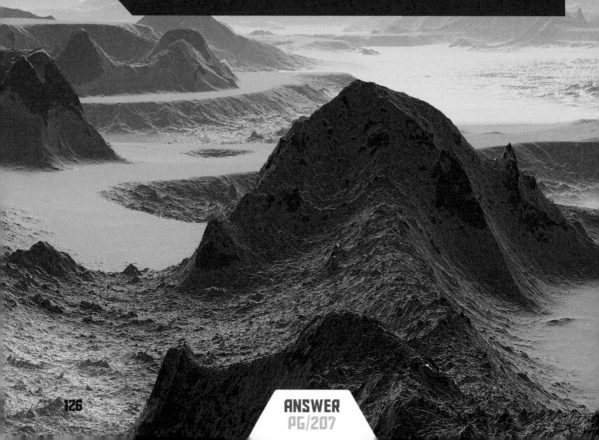

SHADOW

Of all the many lessons learned by the archmage Ged, known as Sparrowhawk, one of the most critical is the requirement for balance between light and darkness. Without one, the world burns; without the other, it freezes. Day and night are a vital dyad, and there is nothing in darkness to make it intrinsically fearsome. Dawn and dusk may be beautiful, but they are not to be sought to the exclusion of the other.

It's commonly known, on Earth, that it takes light eight minutes to reach us from the Sun. Let us pretend for a moment that it's currently the right time of year so that where you live, dawn tomorrow would normally occur at precisely 6am.

WHAT TIME WOULD THE SUN RISE TOMORROW IF LIGHT ACTUALLY MOVED INFINITELY FAST?

ANSWER
PG/207

PIT

While searching for treasure in the Tombs of the Nameless Ones, on the island of Atuan, the archmage Ged is discovered by the high priestess, Tenar. His magic is unable to help him in this place and he is imprisoned, unable to free himself. Her duty requires her to leave him to starve to death as a sacrifice to the Nameless Ones.

In other places and times, condemned prisoners were sometimes thrown into flask-shaped earth pits dug out of the soil below stone-lined tunnels deep beneath the ground. Although the cell portion of these pits could be as much as 20 feet across and 20 feet deep, the opening at the top was typically no bigger than 3 or 4 feet in diameter. Few people who went into such a cell ever came back out, alive or dead. Many prisoners broke limbs falling in, and even the ones who did not were unable to climb back out, as the walls sloped inward from cell to opening.

Even if a prisoner found themselves in such a cell having managed to smuggle in a digging tool and avoid breaking any bones, they would still be deep underground. Tunnelling out and up to the surface would be vanishingly difficult, particularly on the sorts of meagre food rations the luckiest such prisoners received, and it would not be useful to just breach the pit's walls. So, even with a shovel, there would be no escape.

WOULD THERE?

ANSWER
PG/208

APHASIA

Spoken language is the vibration of air within the throat. What we think of as sound is just changes in air pressure as molecules are forced together or apart. As other molecules around the wavefront are alternately pulled in or pushed away by the pressure changes behind them, the sound propagates. We think of speech as inherently full of meaning but, without the brain to translate the tiny variations of atmospheric pressure into something the mind can recognize, language – all sound – is just atomic chaos.

Similarly, an open bell makes noise when struck with a hammer because the metal of the bell vibrates and, in doing so, it forces the air around it to vibrate – which we perceive as sound. If metal were not an elastic substance, it would just crumple at the impact point and there would be no sound. As it is, it deforms, then springs back toward its previous shape, overshooting slightly into deformity again and again, but less each time, until it returns to stasis and the sound fades.

HOWEVER, METAL IS IMPERFECTLY ELASTIC. WOULD THE BELL RING IF IT AND THE HAMMER WERE BOTH MADE FROM PERFECTLY ELASTIC MATERIALS?

ANSWER
PG/208

MULTIVERSE

Strupsirts is a favourite destination for newer trans-dimensional travellers. Partly, this is because it is easy to find, so almost everybody comes through occasionally. But the region is striking – with its dramatic volcanoes and waterspouts – and the locals are friendly and welcoming to travellers from other times and places. So, it is not uncommon to find yourself in very diverse company, and the oddest people can turn out to know each other.

At an Interplanetary Agency dinner party in Strupsirts, you and your partner find yourselves at a table with eight other guests – five couples in total. Somehow, each of the other nine has previously met a different number of people at the table. One person has met just one other, one has met nine others, and one accounts for each possible number of acquaintances in between. Clearly, couples already know each other, so no one has met nobody before and, if X has met Y, then Y has met X.

HOW MANY OF THE GROUP DID YOU KNOW BEFORE THE PARTY?

ANSWER
PG/210

CORN

Travelling the plains, one might find one's way to Islac – a pleasant, welcoming world occupied by a very varied people. With a little gentle persistence, one might hear references, on the part of the locals, to the Ban. Then, if one is fortunate and of a sympathetic disposition, one might even discover the nature of the Ban. Genetic science leaped up to an entirely new height some years previously, and it became incredibly fashionable to splice one's genome with material from animals, birds or even plants.

When it became clear that perhaps this was not such a wonderful idea, the Ban was instituted, severely restricting those with mutated DNA for the ongoing good of the species. The lack of obvious signs in many cases of hybridization only added to the local paranoia. Visitors, of course, are accorded every courtesy and are free of strictures, so it is still a pleasant place to jaunt to.

Assume that a group of 37 Islai are known to have at least one hybrid person among them. Tests are carried out by comparison to another and, from each pair of individuals you pick, at least one is unhybridized.

WHAT IS THE LEAST NUMBER OF HYBRID PEOPLE POSSIBLE IN THE GROUP?

ANSWER
PG/211

LE GUIN

HOW MUCH DO YOU KNOW ABOUT URSULA K LE GUIN AND HER WORKS?

A. In which US state was Le Guin born?
i. California.   **ii.** Massachusetts.
iii. Ohio.   **iv.** Oregon.

B. The K in Le Guin's name stands for what?
i. Katherine.   **ii.** Keynes.
iii. Kinton.   **iv.** Kroeber.

C. The career of Le Guin's father appears repeatedly as the profession of characters in her fiction – what is it?
i. Aerospace engineer.   **ii.** Anthropologist.
iii. Physicist.   **iv.** Sociologist.

D. In what part of the world is Le Guin's fictional country of Orsinia to be found?
i. Central America.   **ii.** Eastern Europe.
iii. Far East.   **iv.** South-east Pacific.

E. According to Le Guin's primary science-fiction stories, what is the name of humanity's original home planet?
i. Earth.   **ii.** Gethen.
iii. Hain.   **iv.** Seggri.

ANSWER PG/211

F. Which novel won Le Guin both the Hugo and Nebula awards, making her the first woman to achieve this feat?

i. *Planet of Exile.*   **ii.** *The Left Hand of Darkness.*

iii. *Rocannon's World.*   **iv.** *A Wizard of Earthsea.*

G. Le Guin's stories typically refer to telepathy as what?

i. Altai.   **ii.** Direct communication.

iii. Mindspeech.   **iv.** Thought transference.

H. What type of work was Le Guin's first published piece?

i. Joke.   **ii.** Play.

iii. Poem.   **iv.** Short story.

I. A common refrain in early Earthsea stories, later subverted, describes woman's magic as what?

i. Banal.   **ii.** Silent.

iii. Tidy.   **iv.** Weak.

J. Le Guin had a Master's degree and an unfinished PhD in which academic subject?

i. English.   **ii.** French.

iii. Psychology.   **iv.** Sociology.

RAY BRADBURY

1920 - 2012

BRADBURY'S
BIOGRAPHY

RAY BRADBURY'S CREATIVITY AND IMAGINATION AT TIMES APPEARED LIMITLESS – HE PUBLISHED THOUSANDS OF SHORT STORIES OVER THE COURSE OF HIS CAREER WITH AN OVERWHELMING VARIETY OF THEMES, NOT TO MENTION IN A NUMBER OF DIFFERENT GENRES. INDEED, OFTEN BRADBURY MANAGED TO SPAN MORE THAN ONE GENRE IN THE SAME SHORT STORY.

His writing provides vignettes of life in exotic circumstances and locations. His first novel, The Martian Chronicles, is a fine example of this. It is constructed more as a series of short stories telling the tale of Earth's colonization of Mars, and the destruction that ensues, than a more traditional novel. In many ways, the book is a very human series of events that is merely set on an entirely different planet.

In fact, Bradbury did not see his own work as necessarily science-fiction; it was too real for that, in his opinion. Rather, he would take a scientific idea, use it as a platform to explore from, and write from there. Perhaps this is why much of his work deals with the dangers of out-of-control technologies. In what many see as his best work, Fahrenheit 451, he explores a dystopian future in which books are forbidden – surely a nightmare society for Bradbury himself, who wrote every single day of his professional life.

RAY BRADBURY'S BIBLIOGRAPHY

Novels

The Martian Chronicles

Fahrenheit 451

Dandelion Wine

Something Wicked This Way Comes

The Halloween Tree

Death is a Lonely Business

A Graveyard for Lunatics

Green Shadows, White Whale

From the Dust Returned

Let's All Kill Constance

Farewell Summer

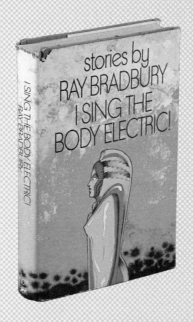

Select Short Story Collections

The Illustrated Man

The Golden Apples of the Sun

The October Country

A Medicine for Melancholy

The Small Assassin

I Sing the Body Electric!

A Sound of Thunder and Other Stories

WELCOMING

When the first exploratory expedition from Earth to Mars touched down, the astronauts were swiftly killed by a jealous local whose wife had telepathically sensed their approach. The Martian authorities were unhappy about the interplanetary risk, and identified and apprehended half-a-dozen suspects, all of whom gave statements. When the detectives in charge investigated, they discovered just one of the six statements was true. Fortunately, that information allowed them to pinpoint the killer.

THE STATEMENTS GIVEN BY THE SIX SUSPECTS CAN BE SUMMED UP AS FOLLOWS:

#1: THE KILLER IS #4.

#2: THE KILLER IS #6.

#3. THE KILLER IS #1.

#4. THE KILLER IS NOT ME.

#5. THE KILLER IS #2.

#6. THE KILLER IS #2.

WHO IS GUILTY?

ANSWER
PG/212

BABE

Alice Lieber is convinced her baby son possesses abnormal abilities, and that he is going to kill her. Her husband, David, and her doctor both try to reassure and comfort her, but a few days later she is dead, having seemingly fallen down the stairs. A couple of days later, the doctor visits the bereaved father and child, and is horrified to discover that David is also dead.

David's death looks like a suicide. His body is slumped over the dining-room table, next to an empty bottle of sleeping pills – the same bottle of 48 pills that the doctor had given the man 36 hours before. There are a couple of the big, oblong pills left lying on the table, but nothing else – no note, no will. Nothing.

THE DOCTOR STUDIES THE SCENE FOR A TIME, AND RELUCTANTLY DECIDES THAT DAVID'S DEATH IS PROBABLY MURDER. WHY?

ANSWER
PG/212

ESCAPE

Having murdered Huxley in a fit of jealous rage, Acton panics. He realizes how much time he's spent at Huxley's home, and how his fingerprints have to be all over the place. He attempts to retrace his movements in order to clean his traces away, but it seems as if everything he wipes down reminds him of three more things that he has to ensure he has sanitized.

When the police finally arrive at the scene, Acton is still there, desperately polishing a bowl of fruit for the third time. Of the items within the bowl, all but two are apples, all but two are plums, and all but two are bananas.

HOW MUCH FRUIT IS IN THE BOWL?

ANSWER
PG/212

THIRD

The third Earth expedition to Mars proves as ill-fated as the first two. The crew arrive to discover a small, picture-perfect American town populated with their dead relatives and long-lost friends. Unfortunately, it's a telepathic illusion and, as soon as the astronauts are off guard, they are killed by the Martians pretending to be their loved ones.

The three expeditions were aimed to land widely spaced from each other across the face of Mars.

WHAT'S THE PROBABILITY OF ALL THREE EXPEDITIONS LANDING WITHIN ONE HEMISPHERE OF THE PLANET'S SURFACE, ASSUMING THE BOUNDARY BETWEEN HEMISPHERES IS NEGLIGIBLY THIN?

ANSWER
PG/214

FLIP

When the fourth expedition from Earth arrives on Mars, they discover that the native Martians have been wiped out. One of the earlier expeditions brought chickenpox with it, and it proved lethal to the Martians. All that remains of their civilization is infrastructure – cities, roads, bridges and so on. Finally, the planet is ripe for human colonization, and not before time, since nuclear war on Earth is looking more and more likely.

Once they know that they are alone, the expedition members start acting out, drinking and gambling, destroying Martian structures, littering the rivers and generally fouling the place. This infuriates the team's archaeologist so much that he starts hunting and killing the rest of the men, hoping that, if he can kill them all, it might just delay a fifth expedition long enough for nuclear war to destroy humanity.

As discipline breaks down, the expedition's captain is forced to resort to a coin toss to send a man out to flank the rogue archaeologist, but even then he is resisted, with the men claiming that the coin could be weighted. Wearily, the captain points out that it's perfectly possible to get a fair either/or result from even the most blatantly biased coin.

HOW?

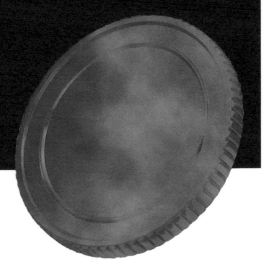

ANSWER
PG/214

NATIVE

Eventually, humans managed to colonize Mars. Sometime shortly after the colonies were established, nuclear war broke out on Earth and contact with the Martian colonies was lost. Once the fighting was done, and the survivors had rebuilt, an attempt was made to get back in contact with the colonists.

Arriving on Mars, the dispatch team discover that the extensive human colonies have been long abandoned, and there is no trace of the people who had lived there. Despite their concerns, the local Martians seem friendly, if a little odd, and they assure the team that they did not harm the humans.

The team are offered the services of one of three possible liaisons for the duration of their visit. The oldest of the trio will always speak truthfully, the youngest will always lie, and the one in the middle will either speak truth or lies at random. There is no visible clue as to which is which, and the team is not given this information. Instead, they are permitted to ask one of the trio a single "yes or no" question, after which they have to make their decision. Once the team has picked someone, they will be informed which one is working with them. Obviously, the honest liaison is the best option, but the liar would also be acceptable, since an obligate liar is still an excellent source of information.

WHAT QUESTION DO THEY ASK?

ANSWER
PG/216

TRANSFORMATION

Inevitably, humanity eventually manages to eradicate the native Martians completely, and begins the process of terra-forming the red planet. One colonist, Ben Driscoll, decides to make it his personal quest to plant a huge forest of carefully adapted trees, hoping to increase the levels of oxygen in the atmosphere. He breaks ground on a large, empty plain one evening and plants a pair of trees as a symbol of his quest.

The Martian soil has unusual properties when brought into contact with Earth plants, and Driscoll expects the trees to duplicate themselves, given sufficient time, and for them and their replicas to then go on to duplicate again. He estimates that the process will take weeks but, the next morning, when he returns to the plain, he discovers that this duplication has taken place not once, but 20 times.

WITHOUT FALLING BACK ON A CALCULATOR, CAN YOU ESTIMATE HOW MANY TREES THERE NOW ARE ON THE PLAIN?

ANSWER
PG/216

TEECE

When the USA's entire population of African-descended citizens decides to emigrate to Mars, many of their regular antagonists are furious at being deprived of both their outlet for malice and their underpaid labour. One, Samuel Teece, goes as far as to attempt to detain as many of the departees as possible, on the flimsiest of pretexts. In the end, he is forced by those close to him to relent.

The other members of the Teece family do not share Samuel's bigotry. In addition to his parents, Samuel has an older and a younger brother, and each of the three brothers has a sister.

HOW MANY SIBLINGS DOES SAMUEL HAVE?

ANSWER
PG/216

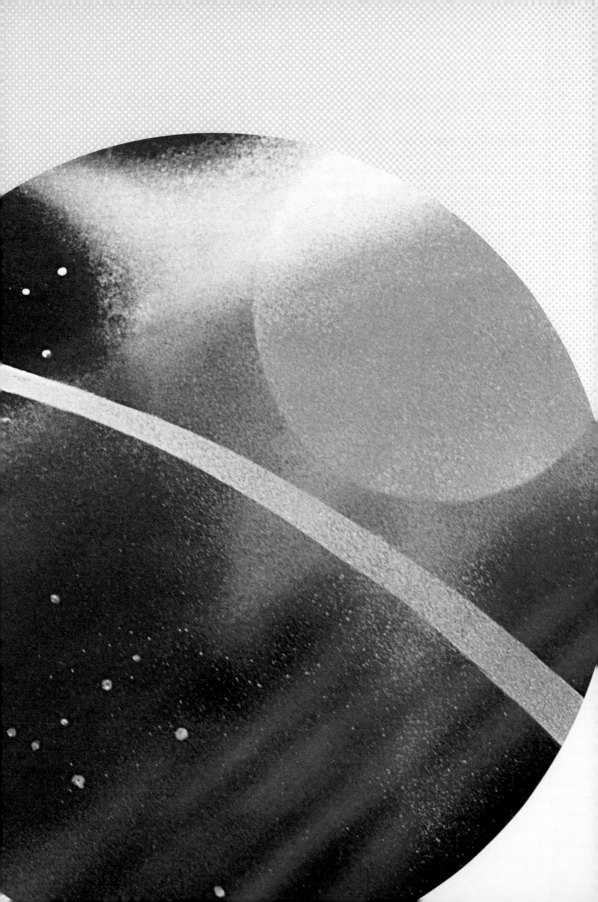

ELECTRICIANS

When the native Martians died off, they left cities behind. In time these fell into ruin, as all things do. When there was little left but bones and walls and odd corners, the children of the new Earth colonies moved in to play and pretend – and destroy.

In one broken dwelling, a little less ravaged than some, a group of children found an intact filament light bulb in a closed room, and a bank of three switches in the wall a short way down the open, partly crumbled hallway. One of the switches turned the light on, so they decided to turn it into a game.

The aim of the game was to figure out which switch powered the light bulb, but it had to be a challenge. So the rules were that you could flick any switches you liked while the door was closed and you couldn't see the result, but then you had to go to the room and say which switch controlled the light.

HOW DO YOU TELL FOR CERTAIN?

ANSWER
PG/217

USHER

Following the rise of the Moral Climate Monitors on Earth – and the horrendous levels of censorship that ensue – William Stendahl retreats to Mars and, with the help of a friend, designs a huge haunted mansion in the style of Poe's House of Usher. The mansion is filled with death-traps of every sort, and the pair even use vast amounts of plant-killer to blight the surrounding landscape. Then they let it be known, dishonestly, that they had a vast hoard of literature and film in there.

As hoped, Moral Climate inspection teams are drawn out to the house and, one by one, they fall prey to the traps, each styled in ways associated with masterpieces of horror. Had the victims known their culture, they could have been safe.

Imagine that you have been captured and placed, completely naked and prone, at the centre of a very large, flat and perfectly frictionless plane of force similar in shape to a huge table. There is nothing in reach, and you are unable to push or pull yourself, because there is no way to grip. In fact, you can't even stand. No one is going to help you.

IS THERE ANY WAY TO GET OFF THE FORCE FIELD?

ANSWER
PG/217

GRIPP

Walter Gripp is one of the last people left on Mars after the collected colonies return to Earth. As a result of certain entirely self-inflicted misadventures, he flees from a deserted colony town. In his haste, he boards an automated bus, only for the controlling machinery to break down, leaving him stuck on a transport that is trundling out of control across the flat, featureless Martian landscape at a steady 30mph. Despite his best efforts, he can't get the bus to stop. The best he can do is open the doors.

Rather than end up being stranded somewhere, perhaps hundreds of miles from any water, food or shelter, he decides that he has to jump while the town is still at least visible on the horizon.

WHAT'S THE BEST DIRECTION FOR GRIPP TO JUMP?

ANSWER PG/218

ICE

Martian colonist LaFarge is surprised to find his son, Tom, outside their home one evening, because Tom has been dead for years. Although LaFarge's wife uncritically welcomes Tom in, the old man is less indiscriminate. After some discussion, LaFarge discovers that Tom is a native Martian with mental powers that make him take the physical and mental form of the couple's dead son.

Tom has many useful insights to share with LaFarge and his wife to help them deal better with the Martian landscape. As an example, during a cold snap, he notices LaFarge is a bit unsteady on his feet when faced with icy patches. He recommends that, rather than try to stick to patches of ice with some grip to them, the old man should do his best to walk on the flattest, slickest patches that he can find.

WHY WOULD THIS BE?

ANSWER
PG/218

ROCKETS

When another round of nuclear wars breaks out on Earth, an extended family manages to steal a rocket from the government and use it to head to Mars. By this point, the planet has been scoured of native Martians and has, subsequently, been settled and abandoned by humans. The family pick one of the abandoned settler cities, land there and scuttle the rocket so that they will not be tempted to return. As part of their ritual for settling in, they pool their passports, tax-ID documents, government paperwork and the like, and burn them together around a campfire. The last thing to burn is a map of the Earth, to mark their new home.

Of course, individual relationships between members of an extended family can become a tangled mess over time, particularly when documentation has been destroyed.

WHAT IS THE MOST DIRECT RELATIONSHIP THAT YOU COULD HAVE TO THE BROTHER-IN-LAW OF YOUR MOTHER'S BROTHER?

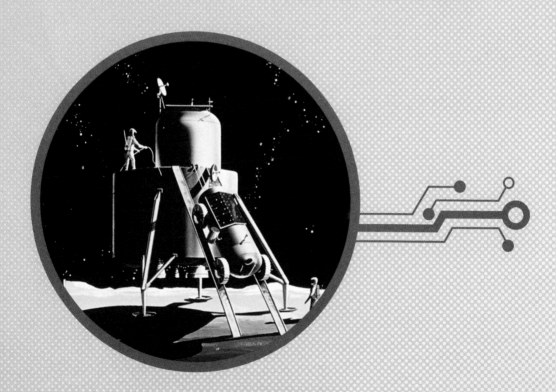

ANSWER PG/220

MONSTER

There's a sea monster outside McDunn's lighthouse, based at a nearby small, rocky island. This initially worries McDunn's young assistant, Johnny. However, the monster does not actually ever attack the lighthouse – it stops short, wailing. McDunn's theory is that the monster has heard the foghorn and thinks that it has found another of its kind. He suggests that, to get it to be quiet and stop wailing, he should just turn off the foghorn and be done with it.

Johnny is concerned that this might anger the monster and lead it to attack them. To help relax him, McDunn points out the thick chain fastened around the monster's neck, too strong for it to break. He's been watching carefully, and the chain is just 90 metres long. The island is well over 150 metres away.

When McDunn turns off the foghorn, the monster goes berserk, as Johnny feared. Although McDunn is correct about the chain, the monster still charges up to the lighthouse and destroys it.

HOW?

ANSWER
PG/220

BELONGING

Guy Montag's straightforward existence is disrupted when he meets his new neighbour, Clarisse McClennan. Most of society is illiterate and hedonistic, and he's part of the reason why. As a fireman, his job is to locate books, which are illegal, and burn both them and the houses they were found in. Talking to Clarisse, he discovers her curiosity and freedom of thought, and begins to realize how narrowly straightjacketed he has become.

When Clarisse and her family disappear, Montag is left pondering many of the things that they spoke about, including the ways that patterns of thought can be restricted. For example, consider three sets of numbers:

A: 36, 60, 89

B: 23, 54, 91

C: 17, 44, 74

TO WHICH GROUP DOES THE NUMBER 16 BELONG?

ANSWER
PG/220

LIGHT

Montag and his colleague, Beatty, are in the firehouse late one rainy night when a call comes in identifying a secret reader. Mrs Phelps reports that she was, just a moment ago, in her parlour, watching her parlour wall screen when she happened to glance out of the window. On the other side of the garden fence, she spotted her neighbour standing sheltered under a large tree at the back of his garden. The man was supposed to be out of town, and the house has, indeed, appeared to be empty for a few days. Now she feels certain that it was a ruse, which strongly suggests that he's been using this time to hide at home, reading.

That sort of secretive behaviour is certainly deeply suspicious. The fire alarm sounds, and Montag, Beatty and the rest of the firemen race over to the address. As the team break in and start ransacking the place for any sign of literature or other forbidden material, Montag realizes that, one way or another, Mrs Phelps was lying.

WHY?

ANSWER PG/221

EXILE

After Montag escapes from his former fireman colleagues, he joins the drifters, a group of former intellectuals who live in the wilderness, away from the oppression of the regime. Shortly after he gets there, the long-expected war breaks out, and the city is destroyed by a nuclear bomb. The whole regime, in fact, is obliterated.

The leader of the exiles, Granger, has long been teaching his people to memorize books so that, when society falls, they can help to rebuild it. Once the dust is settled, Montag and the exiles start making their way back to the city, to help any survivors and start the long, slow process of rebuilding.

On the journey back, Montag gets talking to the other exiles and is startled when one of them tells him that Granger's father was very old when he was born – older than his grandfather, in fact.

HOW?

ANSWER
PG/221

CARNIVAL

Cooger & Dark's Pandemonium Shadow Show is a travelling carnival full of sinister mysteries and strange individuals. It arrives in Green Town in the dead of night, and quickly has the town buzzing with its unseasonal appearance and unusual demeanour. Young teenage friends Will Halloway and Jim Nightshade are fascinated by the carnival and the things it hints at. The merry-go-round appears to be able to rejuvenate or age people and, if the experience of the boys' teacher, Miss Foley, is anything to go by, the mirror maze is particularly horrible.

Of course, normal mirrors are strange enough, in their own way. When you look in a mirror, your image appears to be reversed left to right, but not up to down. If you close your right eye, your image closes its left eye. This is something we all know and take for granted, but it's not as simple as it might seem.

THE LIGHT IS GOING BETWEEN YOU AND THE MIRROR IN A STRAIGHT LINE, AND YOU CAN ROTATE THE MIRROR CLOCKWISE OR ANTI-CLOCKWISE WITHOUT CHANGING YOUR REFLECTION. IS YOUR IMAGE ACTUALLY REVERSED AT ALL?

ANSWER
PG/222

TYGERS

Planet 7 in Star System 84 is billions of miles from Earth. Unlike most exoplanets, it is uncommonly beautiful – soft green hills, delightful forests, clear blue lakes, gentle winds and mile after mile of lush, lovely grass. Enchanted back to his childhood, Driscoll, one of the younger crewmen, asks the wind to lift him in flight and, to everyone's amazement, it does. Soon they are all flying, even Chatterton, the mineral-extraction specialist whose rapacious company is financing the exploration.

Despite Chatterton's increasingly desperate hostility to the planet, it seems to provide them with a river of fine French wine to drink, and even deposits some fish into a boiling spring to give them something to eat. When the mineralogist attempts to bore-drill into the planet in search of useful ore, the drill sinks into a hidden tar pit. Maddened, he tries to use a nuclear bomb against it but, before he can do so, he is apparently devoured by tigers.

The crew are forced to accept that the world is deliberately defending itself from harm, but making itself a paradise for those of them who can appreciate its beauty. The expedition's captain, Forester, orders the crew back onto the ship, blasts off and, in his report, describes the planet as a lethally dangerous hellhole without any exploitable resources.

WHY?

ANSWER
PG/223

BRADBURY

HOW MUCH DO YOU KNOW ABOUT RAY BRADBURY AND HIS WORKS?

A. Without referring back, which decade was Bradbury born in?
i. 1900s.
ii. 1910s.
iii. 1920s.
iv. 1930s

B. Bradbury was a long-time resident of which US state?
i. Alaska.
ii. California.
iii. Illinois.
iv. New York.

C. Mary Bradbury, Ray's direct ancestor, was convicted of which capital crime?
i. Murder.
ii. Spying.
iii. Treason.
iv. Witchcraft.

D. What type of writing was Bradbury's first professional sale?
i. Joke.
ii. Play.
iii. Poem.
iv. Short story.

E. As a teenager, Bradbury was known for being enthusiastic about which hobby?
i. Autograph hunter.
ii. Map-maker.
iii. Modeller.
iv. Plane spotter.

ANSWER PG/223

F. How many Hugo and Nebula SF awards did Bradbury and his works receive?

i. 0. **ii.** 1.

iii. 2. **iv.** 3.

G. Fahrenheit 451 is supposedly the temperature at which what happens?

i. Ink boils. **ii.** Lead type melts.

iii. Leather chars. **iv.** Paper combusts.

H. *The Martian Chronicles* illustrate the moral issues surrounding which area of human group endeavour?

i. Adaptation. **ii.** Colonization.

iii. Industrialization. **iv.** Warfare.

I. The title *The Illustrated Man* refers to which type of illustration?

i. Drawings. **ii.** Graffiti,

iii. Paintings. **iv.** Tattoos.

J. The android surrogate in *I Sing the Body Electric* is intended to fill which family role?

i. Aunt. **ii.** Grandmother.

iii. Mother. **iv.** Sister.

ANSWERS

ISAAC ASIMOV
ANSWERS

ROBOT ^{PG} 13

The new robots do not know about the radiation tests. Take each of the robots in turn to a testing room, one where the gamma source has been disabled, and order them to start the test. Those who are new do not know there is any harm in the tests, and will obey. The rogue does not know the source is disabled, and believes that taking the action to turn the source on will cause harm. Its programming still forbids it from harming a human through its direct action. It is therefore unable to obey.

MARS ^{PG} 14

If the pairs of gloves are X and Y, each has two surfaces, I for original inside and O for original outside. Surgeon A puts on pair X, exposing XI to themselves, then pair Y over the top of them, and operates, with the patient exposing YO. Both pairs are removed. Surgeon B puts on just pair Y, exposing YI and touching the patient with YO, but the patient was the one who exposed YO to begin with, so there is no extra danger. Afterwards, the gloves are again removed. Finally, pair X is turned inside out, and Surgeon C puts them on, exposing XO, which has so far been kept sterile, and then puts pair Y on over the top of them. The patient is once again exposed to YO, which is still no extra danger.

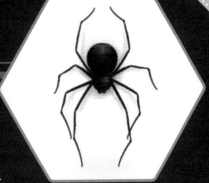

WIDOWERS  ^{PG 16}

His statement, "I did not take the cash or the bonds," is absolutely accurate. He did not take the cash or the bonds. He took the cash **and** the bonds.

ALIENS ^{PG 17}

There are vast numbers of possible reasons why we might not be aware of existing advanced alien life in the galaxy – so many that it's impossible to compile an exhaustive list. We know nothing of the potential progress of life and civilization on other planets. However, most possible reasons why they aren't here involve breaking one of the core assumptions involved in the Fermi Paradox. Any of these would be acceptable answers:

1. We can't recognize alien activity. (They would have to be visible.)

2. The last century or so is not a significant timescale. (They could have visited in the past.)

3. Human knowledge of alien life is being kept secret. (They're not secretly here.)

4. Our solar system is not freely accessible to explore. (We're not in a zoo, for example.)

5. Aliens don't know we're here, or are not curious. (They'd have to know to come here.)

6. Space travel is not easy enough to be worthwhile. (They'd have to be faster than light.)

7. Aliens don't want to expand and explore limitlessly. (They'd need to think like us.)

ISAAC ASIMOV
ANSWERS

LOGIC PG 18

The completed table contains 3 ones, 2 twos, 3 threes, 1 four and 1 five.

Since there five spaces for digits, as well as five digits already in place, the total of the numbers in the blank space column must total to 10. Try inserting all 1s. It's clearly false, but totaling the numbers in the table shows you 6 ones, and one each of the other four. So try again with 6 1 1 1 1. This is still false, but the numbers there now total to 5 1 1 1 1. Try these new figures in place, and they total to 5 1 1 1 2; this then goes to 4 2 1 1 2; on to 3 3 1 2 1; and finally to 3 2 3 1 1, which is accurate.

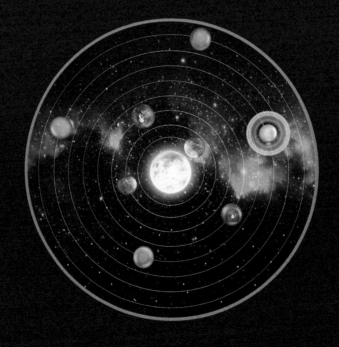

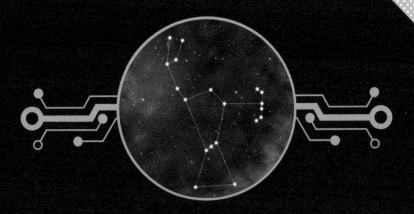

SOLAR PG 19

Our galaxy is moving through the universe at a speed of about 350 miles per second. It is also spinning around its own centre, and the Sun, being in one of the spiral arms, is revolving around that point at about 140 miles per second. The planets are drawn along with the Sun, so our path is a very long, stretched-out spiral, running with the Sun at unfathomable speeds.

Your precise location at this moment one year ago now lies outside our solar system – roughly **15 billion** miles away.

EMPIRICAL PG 20

Although the stars that make up each constellation appear close to each other in Earth's skies, that is just an accident of perspective. In actuality, they can be unimaginably far apart – some are even distant galaxies. They appear close just because of the spot we're looking from. In different star systems, the patterns we know now are simply not there to be found.

ISAAC ASIMOV
ANSWERS

PULL _{PG 21}

It's not possible, unless you find a way to move to a completely different universe. Although in practice the actual pull of the Earth is incredibly close to zero at large distances, gravity has limitless range. Everything that exists is pulling imperceptibly on everything else, all the time.

BELT _{PG 22}

Honestly, it's still not any sort of problem. You just go around it. Before it coalesced into a star, the Sun was a spinning disc of matter, and so the planets – and the asteroid belt – formed within the plane of that disc. To oversimplify, the asteroid belt is flat, at least in astronomical terms. You have to go a bit further, but if you do you can just go above or below it – it's fairly trivial to bypass it entirely.

AZAZEL ^{PG 23}

Azazel stole Picasso's signatures off the paintings, flake by flake.
Unsigned, the paintings became no better than fakes.

VESTA ^{PG 24}

One of the men put on the spacesuit and melted a hole in the outside
of the water tank, angling it so that, as the water escaped into space,
the corresponding reaction would push them towards the surface of the
asteroid.

SILICONY PG 27

The silicony did not draw any particular distinction between its home asteroid and the freighter. Both were small objects that moved through space. Urth figured this out, and discovered the coordinates of the uranium deposit etched onto the hull of the *Robert Q*.

GOOSE ^{PG 28}

Put the goose in a climate-sealed environment and filter the oxygen-18 out of the air – if necessary, using the goose to convert it. There will still be plenty of regular oxygen for it to breathe. Once the air is clear of oxygen-18, the eggs will be gold-free, and thus viable.

HENRY ^{PG 29}

Anderson's peace of mind.

PAPER ^{PG 30}

He instructed the professor on which questions to put on the exam *before* the paper was compiled – and paid him handsomely for it. There was no need for the professor to reveal anything to him at any time, as Lance was the originator of the questions.

ISAAC ASIMOV
ANSWERS

MAYOR PG 32

There is no law forbidding a robot from harming another robot. If the heckler is also a human-seeming robot, Byerley could easily punch him without violating the First Law.

PAST PG 33

As the agent points out, the past begins the tiniest instant before the present. The chronoscope is the perfect spy device, able to see into every home, meeting room and secret facility with complete clarity. The device has completely eliminated any hint of privacy from the world, turning it into a voyeur's paradise.

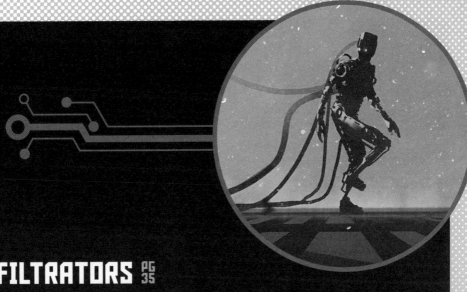

INFILTRATORS ^{PG 35}

He immediately kills the secret agent. The only way that the infiltrator robots could have known of the screening is if news of it had been transmitted directly to them, and the agent is the only candidate.

As the agent's body slumps, it leaks oil rather than blood, confirming that he, too, was a replacement.

CONFLICT ^{PG 36}

Donovan placed himself in life-threatening danger within sight of Speedy. The First Law overrides the Second and Third, and so the conflicting imperatives were suspended. Speedy returned to rationality, rescued Donovan, and while he was doing so, was instructed about the true importance of the selenium, leaving him able to fetch it so as to keep the station's life support running.

ASIMOV ^{PG 38}

A. iv, Russia.

B. iii, New York.

C. iii, Flying.

D. ii, Philosophy.

E. i, Enclosed spaces.

F. i, Susan Calvin.

G. iv, Psychohistory.

H. iii, Radioactive.

I. ii, Mystery.

J. ii, Lucky.

ROBERT A HEINLEIN
ANSWERS

STOBOR ^{PG 45}

By warning the trainees about something that they cannot possibly know anything about, they are put on their guard against the unknown, and primed to treat the alien wilderness they are sent to with the caution it deserves.

TWINS ^{PG 46}

Time passes more slowly when you travel near to light-speed. Although from Tom's point of view it is the Earth that is moving away, an external observer would see the Earth – and Pat – still moving at the usual 500,000+ mph, just 1/3000th of light speed. Pat, staying on Earth, will age faster.

There are two main theories as to why time will pass more slowly for Tom and the torch-ship, a phenomenon known as "time dilation". Albert Einstein suggested that it was the acceleration to light-speed, interacting with the universe's gravitational fields, that produced the time dilation. The other broad class of theories suggest that the multiplicity of inertial frames experienced by the body at light-speed make the space-time paths of the Earth and the spaceship non-symmetrical, resulting in the time dilation.

GRAND PG 47

Infinity is, by its nature, unlimited – the idea of an end to it is meaningless. The slow, simple way is to ask each current guest to move from their current room to the next room along, book in one new guest in room 1, and then repeat infinitely. A faster option would be to ask every current guest to move to the room whose number is twice as large as their current room, opening up an infinite amount of odd-numbered rooms for the new arrivals. But there are literally an infinite number of ways to assign the new rooms. The thing they all share is the deeply counter-intuitive truth that infinity plus infinity is still only infinity.

FAMILY PG 48

If Diana is Carrie's third cousin once removed, Carrie's great-grandmother was the sister of Diana's great-great grandmother. Tracing that down a couple of generations, Diana's grandmother, Anne, was second cousin to Carrie's mum, Betsy, and so second cousin once removed to Carrie, and second cousin twice removed to little Robert.

ROBERT A HEINLEIN
ANSWERS

DUST ᴾᴳ 50

Clark planted the package in his sister's luggage, and then made an antagonistic fool of himself to distract the customs officers, so that his sister and uncle would escape attention.

GRAVITY ᴾᴳ 51

Spin the spaceship along its axis. The centrifugal* force generated is identical in nature to gravity. Getting it to match Earth's standard gravity is just a matter of fine-tuning the rotation and the location of the crew's habitats. The force is strongest furthest from the centre, so the heart of the ship will still be without any apparent gravity, but as long as the crew spend most of the time in their usual gravity, they'll be fine physiologically.

As an aside, accelerating the spaceship in a straight line at the same rate as Earth's standard gravity would provide apparent gravity pulling toward the rear of the ship. This is fine for short journeys, but over time the ship will start approaching light-speed and have to stop accelerating as its mass increases, and so the apparent gravity will fail.

*At the risk of getting arcane, centrifugal force doesn't really exist – it's a shortcut term for an expression of inertia that arises in response to the reactive force keeping the spinning matter from flying away from the point of rotation, as seen from within an internal frame of reference to that rotation.

CURIOSITY ^{PG 52}

The chromosomes in their parental egg and sperm were, effectively, each divided into two halves, each half containing 50% of each parent's DNA. Those halves were recombined into pre-embryos and implanted into a surrogate mother. The resulting babies were referred to as "mirror twins". It is normal for a child to have an even mix of genes from mother and father, but the probability of two siblings having exactly opposite complementary genetic blends is so small as to be functionally impossible in nature.

LUX ^{PG 53}

They lay open the details and schematics of the device to all and sundry, requesting only a small royalty in return. This allows everyone to generate as much electrical power as they need, ruining the Syndicate.

TRIFLE ^{PG 54}

If you guessed under 10km, well done. The actual answer is that it will just about make 4km. We think of the air around us as insubstantial because we are (almost) always within it, but that impression is very far from the truth. This illustrates the complexities Libby was consistently faced with.

ROBERT A HEINLEIN
ANSWERS

ROLLING PG 56

The technicians all had detailed psychological evaluations, and Van Kleeck had access to all their files. Using that information, he broke them down into groups who could be motivated in similar ways, got them together, and worked directly on their particular prejudices and weaknesses.

It's a remarkably effective technique.

ROUTING PG 57

Forget how many possible locations there are on a network; the only ones that factor into this problem are the ones you need to visit. These effectively make up your personal network for the trip. Each destination you add to a network increases the number of possible routes exponentially. Specifically, if you are adding the xth destination, you are multiplying the previous number of possible routes by x. So, if you have one destination, there is one route. Two destinations gives two routes, because $1 \times 2 = 2$. Three destinations give six routes ($1 \times 2 \times 3 = 6$). Four give twenty-four routes, and so on.

Just finding the most effective route between 60 destinations – a perfectly feasible day's work for a single van courier – requires the analysis of approximately as many routes as there are atoms in the entire universe (8×10^{81}).

SCUDDER ᴾᴳ 58

The custodian lied to him – another
car was in the car park for several hours,
long enough for the rains to come and go,
leaving a dry spot where it had been parked.
The deception makes it probable that he's one
of the Prophet's spies.

CAPTIVITY ᴾᴳ 59

Yes, he has a two-thirds chance of getting through safely. Call the
correct door X, the untrapped storeroom door Y, and the trapped
storeroom door Z. There are six possible orders he can open the doors
in. In two of the six, he starts with X, and escapes in 10 minutes. If
he starts with Y, and then moves to X, he escapes in 20 minutes. If
he starts with Z and then moves to X, X will take longer, but he'll still
escape in 25 minutes. It's only if he hits X last that he will be caught – Z
Y X would take 40 minutes, and Y Z X would take 35.

SERVICE ᴾᴳ 60

If the location cannot be moved, and the delegates have to be present,
then the only variable open to adjustment is the gravity itself. So the
company sets to work on developing a form of anti-gravity that can
permit the delegates to remain safe and comfortable on the planet.

ROBERT A HEINLEIN
ANSWERS

DETAILS PG 62

If you guessed somewhere between 20 and 25 years, well done. If you calculated it out, then even better! Laying down $245 a week, it'll take him 1,212 weeks – that's 23 years, 3 months and 21 days – to cover his debt, by which time he'll have paid a total of almost $300,000.

To calculate it precisely, you need to work from compound interest equations. These are usually presented so that they are solving for the amount of your regular payment, but say **N** is the number of payments, **P** is the payment amount, **V** is the value of the original loan, and **i** is the interest rate calculated as a fraction per payment. Then $n = \log(P/(P-Vi))/\log(1+i)$. A rate of 1% interest a month works out at 12.683% a year, which in turn is 0.2298% a week. So, in the equation, i is .002298. P and V are givens: P is 245, and V is 100,000, and multiplying V by i for Vi gives 229.8. Then the number of payments n is $\log(245/15.2) / \log(1.002298)$, which calculates out to 1,211.1 weeks.

ROBERT A HEINLEIN
ANSWERS

SHUTTLE ^{PG 65}

The passenger, Michael. He knows that a locker was opened, despite the captain only asking if he saw anything suspicious.

SUNLIGHT ^{PG 66}

42.41 metres per second, or almost 95 miles per hour. His radius of rotation, **r**, has gone from 100m to 135m, but his angular velocity, Ω, is still 3rpm, so he's moving more swiftly. His tangential velocity **V** is $\Omega \times$ **r**, but to avoid having to factor in constants for conversion from rpm, we want to convert 3 revolutions per minute to the more compatible radians per second. Radians measure angle, so radians per second tell you how quickly something is moving along a circular path. By definition, there are 2π radians in a circle, and one revolution is one full circle of an arbitrary point on the circumference. So 3rpm in 60 seconds is 6π radians, and in radians per second, 6/60ths (or 0.1) π. So $V = 135 \times 0.3142 = 42.41$.

GOVERNOR ^{PG 67}

Just Bob himself. Assume Bob's mother has two brothers. Bob has a brother and sister, and they have married the daughter and son of one of their uncles. Bob himself has previously married, and lost, the daughter of his other uncle. This then can define the four relationships as just one person, the father of his siblings' spouses. If that man dies, and Bob marries his widow, then Bob himself becomes that person.

VACUUM ^{PG 69}

Konski sits on the leak. Between the suit's protective material and his own mass, he is able to effectively plug the gap without fatally injuring himself.

HEINLEIN ^{PG 70}

A. ii, Grok.

B. iv, Waterbed.

C. iv, Navy.

D. iii, Stonemasonry.

E. ii, Anson.

F. iv, *Total Recall.*

G. i, An artificial person.

H. ii, A Harsh Mistress.

I. i, Future History.

J. i, Alternate dimensions.

ARTHUR C CLARKE
ANSWERS

CRISES _{PG 76}

The beacon is a test to search for intelligent, space-faring life developing on Earth. When the scientists finally manage to get through the force field – with "atomic power" – that is taken as proof of intelligence. The beacon therefore stops transmitting, to alert the civilization that left it there. Stopping an ongoing signal is a safer alert method than starting to signal after silence, because no matter what happens to the beacon, or how quickly, the message is still sent.

CRITTER _{PG 77}

The solar radiation. It's an extremely powerful source of energy – more than enough to support properly adapted life.

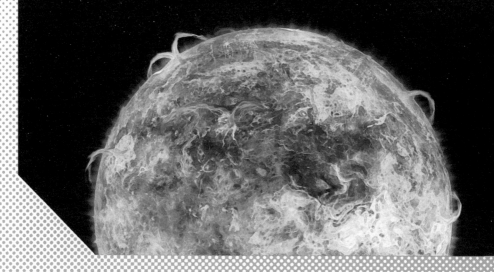

MALICE PG 78

The cosmonaut had access to a tape recorder, and although she wasn't able to respond usefully, she was able to record Tibor's threats and taunts.

DEUS PG 79

The equation to calculate the number of possible permutations, **P**, of a number of elements, **r**, from a larger pool of options of size **n**, is **P** = **n!** / **(n-r)!** – but this can be simplified with a little logical thought.

The term n! is shorthand for $1 \times 2 \times 3 \times$... and so on until ... $\times$ n. If n = 6, then n! = $1 \times 2 \times 3 \times 4 \times 5 \times 6$. So the term (n-r)! means $1 \times 2 \times 3 \times$... $\times$ (n-r). If n = 6 and r = 2, then (n-r) = 4, and (n-r)! is $1 \times 2 \times 3 \times 4$. Which makes n!/(n-r)! into 6! / 4!, or $1 \times 2 \times 3 \times 4 \times 5 \times 6$ / $1 \times 2 \times 3 \times 4$. If an identical term appears on both the top and bottom of a division in this way, you can remove it from both parts. In other words, 6! / 4! = 5×6. This principle holds true for all permutations of this type.

From the question, you know that somewhere around half of the possible permutations of the alphabet are invalid. So, you want a total number of possible permutations, P, that is a little under 18 billion. Further, you know that r, the number of letters in each name, is 9. Practically, this means that if you expand n!/(n-r)! out to a list of $1 \times 2 \times 3$... etc., and cancel out the common terms above and below, your answer actually starts at $10 \times 11 \times 12 \times$... and goes up to n. Rather than delve into complex quadratics, try expanding out on a calculator, term by term. So, $10 \times 11 = 110$; then $10 \times 11 \times 12 = 1,320$; and so on. You'll quickly discover that $10 \times 11 \times 12 \times 13 \times 14 \times 15 \times 16 \times 17 \times 18 = 17,643,225,600$ – a little under 18 billion.

The divine alphabet has 18 characters.

ARTHUR C CLARKE
ANSWERS

ZEUS PG 80

Mount Zeus is, in fact, a shard of Jupiter's solid diamond core that smashed into Europa during the transformation, lodging deep into the new planet.

SKYBIKE PG 83

He takes off his shirt and uses it as a parachute. Between the light gravity and regular atmospheric density, this gives him sufficient lift to land safely at the base of the cliff.

MALFUNCTION PG 84

Hal's orders are to hide the *Discovery*'s true mission from the crew, but this instruction runs contrary to its core programming of discovering and relaying accurate information. Unable to reconcile these two imperatives, it gets increasingly distracted until it decides that the best way to avoid having to lie to the crew is to kill them.

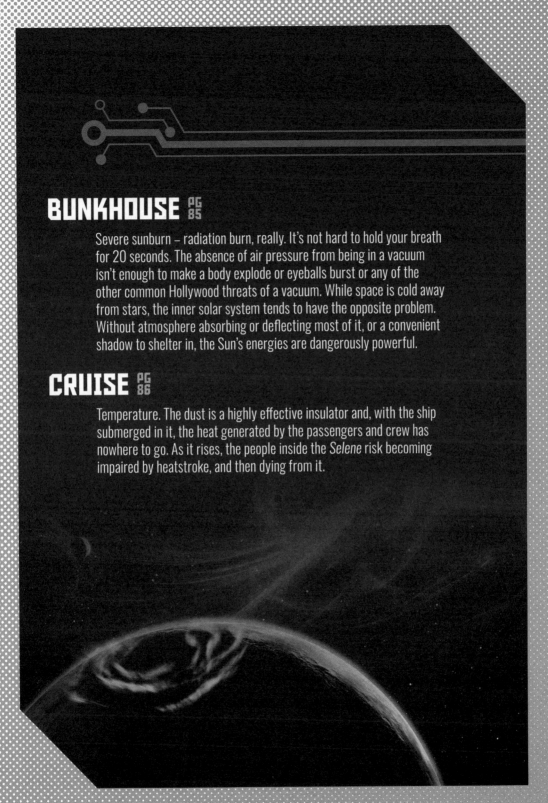

BUNKHOUSE ^{PG 85}

Severe sunburn – radiation burn, really. It's not hard to hold your breath for 20 seconds. The absence of air pressure from being in a vacuum isn't enough to make a body explode or eyeballs burst or any of the other common Hollywood threats of a vacuum. While space is cold away from stars, the inner solar system tends to have the opposite problem. Without atmosphere absorbing or deflecting most of it, or a convenient shadow to shelter in, the Sun's energies are dangerously powerful.

CRUISE ^{PG 86}

Temperature. The dust is a highly effective insulator and, with the ship submerged in it, the heat generated by the passengers and crew has nowhere to go. As it rises, the people inside the *Selene* risk becoming impaired by heatstroke, and then dying from it.

ARTHUR C CLARKE
ANSWERS

INVERTED PG 88

Many critical nutrients, including amino acids, are chiral molecules –
that is, they are not symmetrical in reflection. Since the molecules of
Nelson's body have been reflected, they can now only process similarly
reflected nutrients, which do not naturally exist and cannot easily be
created.

FLYBOY PG 90

The ship belongs to a film studio who are going to be shooting a movie
on and around the station. The items are props.

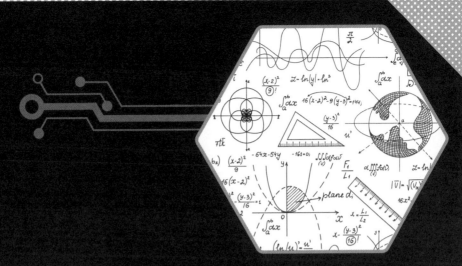

SECRETS PG 91

No. There's a very significant difference between actual average lifespan and theoretical maximum life expectancy – 104, in humans, a figure that hasn't changed in tens of thousands of years. Doubling theoretical maximum life expectancy would have little impact on actual average lifespan. Some countries, such as the USA, do not acknowledge "old age" as a cause of death, but in places where they do, a fatality rate of 8% due to old age is quite typical. In fact, old age doesn't become the most common cause of death until well into the 90s, an age reached only by around 15% of the population. Cancer and heart disease kill more people before then. Even if we assume that somehow anyone getting to 95 then becomes magically immune to cancer and other disease, we'd only be adding 15% to the global population Henry Cooper is used to: a "mere" billion people or so. In practice, those issues would continue killing the very old, so the total population growth would, most likely, only be a few per cent. Real estimates of how many people Earth can indefinitely support range from four billion to ten billion, with the likely actual number being in the six to eight billion range. As of March 2020, there are around 7.8 billion of us.

ARTHUR C CLARKE

ANSWERS

EARLY PG 92

Earth and Jupiter orbit the Sun at very different speeds. At their closest, the planets are a little over 6.25 million km apart; at their furthest, a bit more than 9.25 million km. Launch windows are extremely complex, but the bottom line is that neither ship has sufficient fuel to cover the manoeuvres necessary to make the longer journey back if they leave early. The crews eventually use the *Discovery* as a booster rocket to escape Jupiter's orbit, leaving the *Leonov* with the spare fuel needed to make the longer, more complex trip.

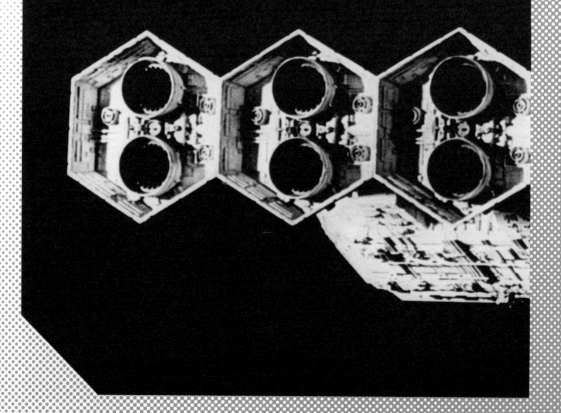

NORTH PG 95

The *Doradus* is piloted by humans, and even well-trained human reflexes require a tenth of a second to respond to an audio cue, and twice that for a visual one. In a tenth of a second, starting from dead still, the *Doradus* would travel 100 metres, and within a full second, it would be moving at over 2,000mph. Its lasers are forward-facing, and its thrusters are orthogonal – it's built for space combat, where enemy vessels are facing the same issues of momentum and manoeuvring that it is. K-15, on the other hand, is on his feet, and even flat out, at 1mph, he has little momentum to worry about. The best the *Doradus* can hope for is a strafing run, and that will only be possible if K-15 is dumb enough to stay going in one direction for an extended period of time. K-15 should be fine.

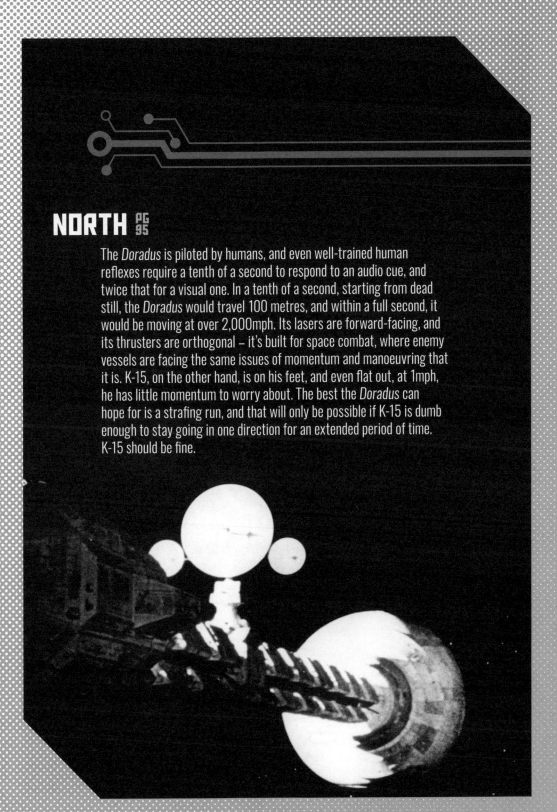

ARTHUR C CLARKE
ANSWERS

VIRAL PG 96

With the failure report requiring 450 years to get back to the aliens and, in every likelihood, their response needing a further 450 years to make it back, Poole expects to be long dead, and there's plenty of time for the species to find strategies to survive.

WEAPON PG 97

At some point, you will reach a threshold where it just won't be worth it for the pain to get worse. Your next jolt will still be OK, it won't be noticeably worse than the previous one, but the one after that will genuinely be measurably worse than the one you just had. So, you need to stop *after* the next activation.

HARRY PG 99

The van was delivering a large shipment of bees to a local beekeeper and had nothing to do with the laboratory. The apparent fluid was the swarm, groggy and confused from having the crates that were housing it destroyed.

CACTUS ^{PG 100}

He was examining the plant when it ejected a seed with sufficient force to smash through his helmet, his eye and his skull. He died instantly.

PERFECT ^{PG 101}

None. Although a hollow sphere attracts objects outside of it as any other mass would do, inside there is no net gravitation attraction. At the centre, it's fairly easy to see why, as every point around you is pulling you equally, and they all negate each other. As you get closer to one point on the inside of the shell, it does exert a stronger effect on you – but that is perfectly cancelled out by the percentage of other points pulling you in the opposite direction.

CLARKE ^{PG 102}

A. ii, British.

C. i, Air force.

E. i, Scuba diving.

G. iv, Polio.

I. iii, *Arthur C. Clarke's Strange World.*

B. iii, Stanley Kubrick.

D. iii, 1:4:9.

F. iv, Third.

H. ii, Sri Lanka.

J. iv, The White Hart.

URSULA K LE GUIN
ANSWERS

ANSIBLE PG 108

After 60 seconds, the ship's speed is infinite – but infinity is not a tangible part of physical reality. "Infinitely far away" is meaningless, because any real location in space-time that it is possible to be at is, by definition, not infinite. So, the answer really depends on the universe. If reality extends infinitely, the ship is outside of reality, best described as "nowhere". If reality does not extend infinitely but instead wraps back on itself (the current best guess of experimental physicists), then the ship is moving through all of the universe simultaneously, best described as "everywhere".

This is, of course, impossible.

BEQUEST PG 109

Although she has, indeed, only spent two days in travel, she's spent that time just below light-speed. The museum is 10 light years from Fomalhaut and, as far as the universe is concerned, she has been gone for 20 years.

EMBARGO PG 110

The League's enemies are already established on Fomalhaut II, and have been for some time. They destroy Rocannon's ship, taking out his ansible in the process. With the planet under embargo, no one is going to check on him or come to his aid.

SHING PG 111

The Shing want to restore his memories because he has information they want – specifically, as it turns out, the location of his home planet, which Orry was too young to know.

FORETELLING PG 112

The chance is 20%. The two red balls are a pair of unique items. There are 12 possible ways to draw two out of Blue, White, Red 1 and Red 2. We know that there is one red already, so Blue/White and White/Blue are ruled out. That leaves 10 possibilities. Of those 10, only Red 1/Red 2 and Red 2/Red 1 give you two red balls. 2/10 is 20%.

URSULA K LE GUIN

ANSWERS

WALLS ^{PG 113}

Sitting in this way, your centre of gravity is aligned with your spine, but the power to lift up comes from your thighs and calves, which are rooted in your feet. The distance between the centre of gravity and point of pressure is just too great. You will not be able to stand until you bring them closer by leaning forward and/or bringing your feet back.

FEAR ^{PG 114}

Although each plant is simple in itself, it is part of a unified consciousness – a single mind that uses its individual components the way our brains use individual neurons. The fear didn't follow them; the consciousness is unitary, so it is everywhere on the planet. It is terrified by the arrival of external life that is not part of itself.

YEARS PG 116

Laia is 80. To solve this, we need to convert the fractional proportions of lifespan to a common denominator so they can be compared. There are several possible denominators, but one will be her correct age: X. Her time in decline, 14 years, can also be very simply converted to a fractional proportion of her correct age, just by writing it as 14/X. So we have 1/8, 1/5, 1/2 and 14/X. We know these add up to her full age, so, when all the fractions are expressed with her true age as the denominator, the four numerators will also add up to X – or mathematically, 1/8 + 1/5 + 1/2 + 14/X = X/X = 1.

The lowest common denominator of 8, 5 and 2 is 40, so start by multiplying the top and bottom of each known fraction by the number required to turn the denominator into 40. We can't safely change X, because we don't know what it is. So, multiply 1/8 by 5, 1/5 by 8, and 1/2 by 20, to turn our equation into 5/40 + 8/40 + 20/40 + 14/X = 1. So, is she 40? Test by adding the numerators: 5 + 8 + 20 + 14 = 47. As 47 does not equal 40, she's not 40. We're 7 over, which is half of 14, so with an age of 40, 14/X is twice what we need it to be. That means we need to double 40 to make it balance, since we can't change X. So multiply all the known fractions by 2 to double them. Then we get 10/80 + 16/80 + 40/80 + 14/X = 1. Test again. Yes, 10 + 16 + 40 + 14 = 80, and so 10/80 + 16/80 + 40/80 + 14/80 = 80/80 = 1.

URSULA K LE GUIN
ANSWERS

WILDER PG 117

Orrec does not have any gift. His father, in the guise of attempting to train him, was using his own power to fake his son's lack of control. Canoc knew his son was powerless, and was trying to make the boy seem terrifying, in order to keep attackers from risking an assault on the domain.

RESISTANCE PG 118

As a woman, Memer is both utterly incapable and beneath notice as far as the Alds are concerned. The idea that a woman could be an actual threat is foreign to them. Provided that she is not caught out on the streets, she will be almost completely safe.

GENERATIONAL PG 120

Usually, a random answer from four possibilities has a 25% chance of being correct. But B and C are both 25%, so the chance of getting 25% of them is actually 50%. D is 50%, but that can't be correct, because there is only a 25% chance of picking it. That would leave you with an irreconcilable paradox, so the real chance is 0% – except that 0% is A, which has a 25% chance of being selected.

Although it looks like a function question, it is not answerable – effectively, it is meaningless.

DRAGONS PG 123

No. Deer taste good, and they're suitable as food, but they whine, so dragons always ignore them because they're boring.

NAMING PG 124

They are among the longest pure anagrams in the English language – they are made up of the same 14 letters, but no letter is in the same position in both words, and no pair of adjacent letters in one word is repeated in the other word.

URSULA K LE GUIN
ANSWERS

DRY PG 125

We know their deaths were very sudden, and the certainty that magic and advanced technology were not involved makes it clear that this was not deliberate murder, but death due to some environmental factor. Lightning and toxic gas are ruled out by the examination. But what we do not know is how long they have been dead, and we are told that the spring flowers are new.

In fact, the pair were out walking during the winter months when they were buried by an avalanche. Engulfed, they suffocated as they froze, and then stayed hidden in the snow pack until after the spring thaw.

SHADOW PG 126

After 6am by some minutes, possibly even by as much as an hour. When the planet rotates so that you experience the dawn, it's moving you into light that is already there, so it doesn't matter whether that light left the Sun eight minutes ago or eight nanoseconds ago. Thus, dawn won't come early.

In fact, because of light's speed through air, it diffracts in our atmosphere, bending round to reach us sooner than if it was going in the perfectly straight lines we imagine. We have all seen the Sun rise over the horizon before – in fact, we have a direct line to it. We only see the exactly correct position of the Sun on the equator at midday. So, depending on latitude, air pressure, pollution, elevation of surrounding terrain and so on, you seem to see the Sun rise quite a bit earlier than it actually does.

If the light moved infinitely quickly, that diffraction would not occur, and dawn would seem to be late. Incidentally, light moving infinitely quickly would not make the Sun infinitely powerful. We would not be crisped. We would see the stars as they are now, however, rather than seeing them as they were thousands, millions or billions of years in the past.

URSULA K LE GUIN
ANSWERS

PIT ^{PG 129}

The prisoner does not have to tunnel from the cell up to the surface to escape, or even from the cell up to the passage from where they were thrown in. They only need to excavate enough earth to make a mound inside the cell that they can use to reach the opening. Tricky to do without risking getting smothered by a cave-in, but far from impossible.

APHASIA ^{PG 130}

If the bell was perfectly elastic, it would not suffer any deformity at the point of impact. The impact would be instantaneous, with all the energy reflected. There would be no vibration and, thus, no sound. The bell and hammer would immediately spring apart, with the hammer's energy at impact divided between them. That might cause an audible shockwave if you hit the bell hard enough, but the bell itself would not ring.

ANSWERS

MULTIVERSE PG 131

Setting yourself aside, the other nine can be referred to by how many other people they knew before, so think of them as 1 to 9. Clearly, 9 knows everyone, including you, because they don't get to count themselves. Just as clearly, 1 knows only one other person – and the only person who knows everyone is 9, so 1 and 9 know each other, and because everyone knows their partner, 1 and 9 are there together. 8 knows everyone apart from 1, so 2 must know 9 and 8. People are in pairs, so 2 and 8 are a couple. The same logic pairs 3 and 7, and 4 and 6. Your partner is 5, not that it matters. Person 4 knows 9, 8, 7 and 6, but that's all. Your partner, 5, also knows 9, 8, 7 and 6, but they can't count themselves, so they don't "know" 5, and they definitely don't know 4. The fifth person 5 knows has to be you. This same logic applies heading back up the more gregarious folks – 6, 7, 8 and 9 can't count themselves, so they have to know you to make up the right number of acquaintances. So, like your partner, you knew 5 people before tonight.

CORN PG 132

One hybrid person. That is the only way to guarantee that any possible pair has at least one unhybridized person.

LE GUIN PG 134

A. i, California.

B. iv, Kroeber.

C. ii, Anthropologist.

D. ii, Eastern Europe.

E. iii, Hain.

F. ii, *The Left Hand of Darkness.*

G. iii, Mindspeech.

H. iii, Poem.

I. iv, Weak.

J. ii, French.

RAY BRADBURY
ANSWERS

WELCOMING ^{PG} 140

There is only one true statement, and #1 and #4 are directly contradictory, so one of them has to be lying and one telling the truth. If #1 is lying and #4 is telling the truth, neither #3 nor #5 are (falsely) accused by someone else, and there is no definite answer shown. So, #4 is lying and #1 is telling the truth, and #4 is the murderer.

BABE ^{PG} 142

There's no glass, jug or other source of liquid. It's highly unlikely that someone would voluntarily dry-swallow 46 large pills, even if they were able to. Therefore, the scene has been staged.

ESCAPE ^{PG} 143

Three items – one of each type specified.

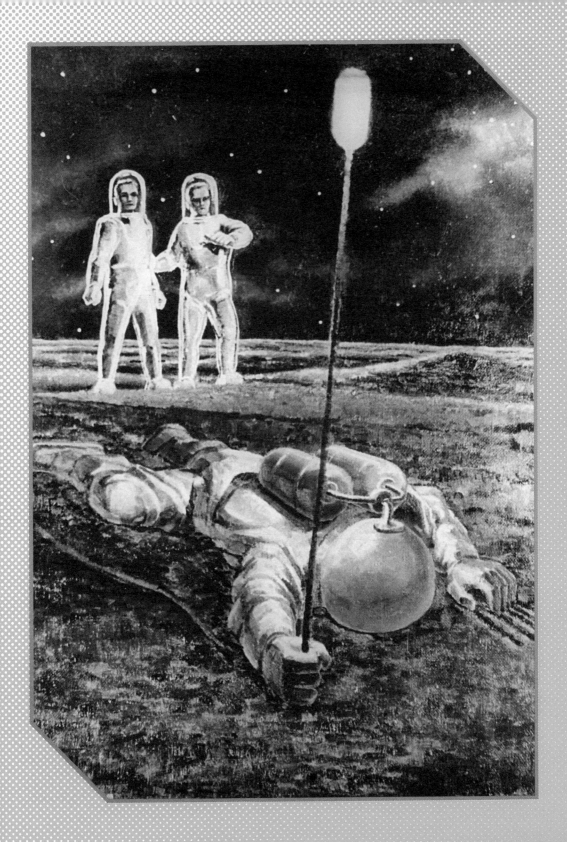

RAY BRADBURY

ANSWERS

THIRD PG 144

100%. The hemisphere in question does not have to align N-S or E-W. If you consider the first two landings as setting a hemisphere boundary, and project that boundary out around the planet, then the third landing has to be on one side or the other, thereby placing all three landings within one half of the planet. Even if you allow the third landing to take place precisely on the vanishingly thin boundary, all you are saying is that the three are together in either of the divisions.

FLIP PG 145

No matter how biased the toss is, a coin will always have exactly the same probability of heads (H) followed by tails (T) as it will of T followed by H. So, throw the coin twice. If it returns HT or TH, that's your answer. If it returns HH or TT, throw it twice more, repeating as necessary.

ANSWERS

NATIVE ^{PG 146}

Since you don't know who is who, let us label the person the team decide to question as "A" and the other two as "B" and "C". The question to ask is, "Is B older than C?" Whatever answer you get, you pick the one who A indicates as younger. If A is the Truth-Teller, you'll get the Liar, as they are younger than the Switch. If A is the Switch, you'll get either the Truth-Teller or the Liar at random. Finally, if A is the Liar, you'll get the Truth-Teller, since they are older than the Switch.

TRANSFORMATION ^{PG 147}

Over a million – 1,048,576 to be precise. The human mind is poor at estimating exponential growth, but if you double a quantity, and keep doubling it, you very quickly start moving into truly enormous numbers.

TEECE ^{PG 148}

Three. Samuel's sister is, of course, the sister to all three of her brothers.

ELECTRICIANS PG 150

Let's call the switches 1, 2 and 3. Start by turning 1 on and leaving it for a while – 15 minutes, say. Then turn it back off, turn on 2 instead, and go into the room. If the light is on, 2 is the right switch. If the light is off but the bulb is hot, 1 is the right switch. If the light is off and the bulb is cold, 3 is the right switch.

USHER PG 152

There is one reliable way to generate some usable force available to you. When you inhale, air enters your nose and mouth from every available angle around them, so it produces very little in the way of net momentum. But when you exhale, your breath is moving in one specific direction, particularly if you purse your lips and breathe out firmly. So, you can gain some momentum by breathing out in such a way, and it will not be reversed when you have to breathe back in. Since you are frictionless, your mass will not impede your movement and you can escape.

ANSWERS

GRIPP PG 153

There are two issues here you want to consider. One is momentum. When you jump off a bus, you are travelling at the same speed it is. The best way to minimize this speed is to jump in the opposite direction to which the bus is travelling. However, the other is the human body's natural functioning. We are far better designed to deal with forward speed than backward speed, and if we fall over forwards, we have hands in place to help break our fall, and our joints are designed to compensate better for the impact than if we fall over backwards. So you want to be facing the direction you are moving when you land. That means the best chance of avoiding a catastrophe is to face forwards, but jump backwards as hard as you can.

ICE PG 155

Despite how it seems, ice is no more slippery than stone, but it melts under pressure, and water is extremely slippery. If the ice is smooth, the pressure of your weight is spread out as widely as possible, and less of it melts underfoot. That makes it a lot less slippery than walking on rough ice, where your weight is concentrated and the ice melts more swiftly. Shoes with unusually wide soles would help even more.

RAY BRADBURY

ANSWERS

ROCKETS ^{PG 156}

It would be your father. He would be at least one of your maternal uncle's brothers-in-law.

MONSTER ^{PG 157}

The chain was fastened around the monster's neck at one end, but the other end was completely loose.

BELONGING ^{PG 158}

Group A is comprised of numbers whose digits are entirely made up of curved lines. Group C is comprised of numbers whose digits are entirely made up of straight lines. Group B is comprised of numbers which include digits with both straight and curved lines. 16, which has a curved digit and a straight digit, belongs with Group B.

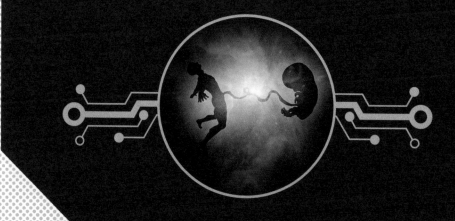

LIGHT PG 160

It's extremely hard to clearly see any unlit area at night from within a lit room. This is doubly the case when it is raining. There's no plausible way that Mrs Phelps could have identified her neighbour under a tree in the back of an unlit garden.

EXILE PG 162

Granger's maternal grandfather was younger than Granger's father.

RAY BRADBURY
ANSWERS

CARNIVAL PG 163

Your mirror image is not reversed left to right, but it is reversed –
front to back. If you were looking not at a mirror but at a hologram of
yourself exactly as you currently are, you'd be looking at the back of
your own head. When you closed your right eye, your hologram would
also close its right eye. This is where the reversal is, in the natural
direction of the light, when it's bounced back to you, so that you see
the front of yourself in the mirror. It's not just your brain helping to
adapt the image, as it does when the Moon is low on the horizon. The
reversal is real. It's just parallel to the mirror, front to back, rather than
perpendicular to it (left to right or up to down).

TYGERS ^{PG 165}

Because while individual people can be careful and respectful, humans as a mass tend to be extremely destructive, spoiling and depleting any shared resource until it is completely destroyed. Their mission is to find worlds to strip-mine for minerals but, even if that fate could be avoided, if the planet's nature was known, it would be overwhelmed and ruined – possibly at great cost to the company as the planet fights back.

BRADBURY ^{PG 166}

A. iii, 1920s.

B. ii, California.

C. iv, Witchcraft.

D. i, Joke.

E. i, Autograph hunter.

F. i, 0.

G. iv, Paper combusts.

H. ii, Colonization.

I. iv, Tattoos.

J. ii, Grandmother.

PICTURE CREDITS

The publishers would like to thank the following sources for their kind permission to reproduce the pictures in this book.